I0721337

# Mountain Refuge
## Misty Hollow

## Cynthia Hickey

# DEDICATION

To all my readers who stayed in Misty Hollow with me.

# Chapter One

"We found her. I've texted the coordinates to your phone. Meet us there ASAP." The line went dead.

Taya Trapp stared at her cell phone. For the first time in months, hope leaped in her chest. Her niece had been found.

Shaking herself into action, she shoved clothing, ammunition, and all the money she'd squirreled away into a camping backpack, along with Mylar blankets and other camping supplies. She knew enough to know that once she had Tracy at her side, they'd have to run. Her niece knew too much about the trafficking ring that took her and her best friend. They'd snatched the girls right from the coffee shop they'd gone to after school.

Once Taya had packed the necessities, she tossed her bag in the back of her Jeep and sped toward the assigned meeting place over an hour away. By the time she drove into the parking lot, lights off, the others had already gathered.

Mason Rogers, night-vision goggles obscuring his features, strode toward her. "This isn't the place. We'll have to move a couple blocks north." He handed her goggles. "You ready?"

"Yes." She donned the goggles and grabbed the automatic rifle from his hand. "Are there others?"

"We believe there to be five other girls besides your niece."

"Great. We'll rescue them all." It wasn't a question.

"If it's in our power to do so, but your niece is our top priority." Without waiting for her response, he dashed back to the group.

Taya agreed, but her conscience wouldn't let her leave any of the innocent behind. She caught up to the others. The group immediately set off at a jog, skirting behind empty warehouses and staying in the shadows.

She fell into the familiar routine of special forces as if she'd never left. After Tracy had been taken, Taya didn't give dropping out a second thought. She knew she'd have to leave once they found her niece.

Mason held up a fist for them to stop, then pointed toward a red-brick, two-story warehouse nestled against the side of a small mountain. Taya took a second to recheck her weapon, then followed close on Mason's heels.

Inside the building, the team split into two lines. Taya went left after Mason. If not for the goggles, they'd all be thrust into total darkness. Now, she saw the world through a green glow. Other than the occasional soft scrape of a shoe, the building remained silent. Her breathing sounded louder than her surroundings. Her heart thrummed in her throat only to slow when she willed it to.

The hall she followed Mason down cut into the mountain. Concrete walls gave way to dirt. A whimper reached Taya's ears.

Mason held up a fist again. They stopped, then inched forward.

They passed cells carved into the mountain. Behind bars huddled teenage girls, their eyes wide. There were many more than the five Mason had mentioned.

Behind Taya, someone shouted an alarm. She whipped around, lowered to one knee, and fired, dropping the first man to step into view. Mason took down the next. Screams from the girls joined the sound of gunfire. From the direction the rest of the team had gone, more gunfire rang out. Taya dropped one clip and jammed in another, barely pausing in her shooting.

When no more men came running toward them, Mason shouted for her to find the key to open the cells. "I don't know how much time we have." He started searching the pockets of the men they'd shot.

Taya plunged her hand into one man's pockets and pulled out a set of keys. "Here." She flipped through the keys until she found one that would fit in the lock. Cell by cell, she unlocked and pulled doors open while Mason gathered the girls against the dirt wall. Tracy was nowhere to be seen.

"She isn't here." Her eyes burned.

"Don't despair. She could be with the others." Mason faced the girls. "Stay close. Stay quiet. Trapp, bring up the rear."

Hope wasn't lost yet. Maybe there were girls on the other side of the warehouse. If Tracy wasn't there, Taya had no clue where she could be. The team would be back at the starting point. No. They were saving a lot of girls. The night wasn't a total waste.

Mason ordered one of the other men to lead the

girls to a van outside before leading Taya in the direction the others had gone. A shot rang out. Mason fell.

Taya spun around and fired in the direction from which the shot had come. Another shot. Her arm burned.

Seconds later, the rest of the team surged forward and joined the fight while a handful of girls were rushed from the building. Taya tried to see if one of them was Tracy, but rapid gunfire kept her attention on sheer survival.

When things died down again, she crawled forward to check on the team leader. Mason stared through his goggles, gone. Tears burned her eyes as two of the team members took him by the arms and dragged him from the building. She started to follow when a voice stopped her.

"Aunt Taya!"

She turned to see Tracy dashing toward her. The girl launched into Taya's arms. Taya wrapped her tightly into a hug, tears spewing from her eyes.

"You're bleeding." Tracy's voice sounded muffled against Taya's chest.

"It's just a graze, baby." A few minutes later, she held Tracy at arm's length. "Did they…?"

"No." Her niece shook her head as extra confirmation. "They were waiting for the highest bidder." She smirked. "Seems there's a lot of money in selling purity."

"We walk from here." Several hours later in which Tracy napped, Taya parked the Jeep behind a closed-down movie rental place.

"How far?" Tracy rubbed her eyes.

"Days." Taya tossed Tracy a backpack stuffed with things her niece would need. "I've mapped out small stores along the way where we can purchase food and water."

"Where are we going?" Her niece frowned and looked at the boots on her feet. "Will these hold up?"

"They should. Cost me enough." Taya shrugged into her pack, shoved her handgun into the waistband of her pants, and grabbed her rifle. "We're headed to a place called Misty Mountain. There's a small town there, but the mountain is heavily wooded. We'll find an abandoned hunter's cabin to stay in for a while."

"Why can't we go to the police?"

"I don't know who we can trust." She set off, staying a few feet behind the trees so a passing vehicle wouldn't spot them. Life wouldn't be easy for quite a while, but as long as Tracy was safe from those whom she could identify, Taya would do anything to keep her safe. Even live off the grid. After an hour of walking, she removed her flannel shirt and tied it around the strap of her pack. "Let's take a five-minute break."

"Thank you, God." Tracy dramatically slumped to the ground and pulled a water bottle from her pack.

Taya smiled, glad to see evidence of a normal teenage girl surface once in a while. After the terror of capture and living six months in a dirt cell, Tracy had a lot of healing to do. Taya would be there to help her for as long as it took.

Dark clouds started to gather overhead, threatening rain. They needed to find a place to take shelter. "Come on. We need to hurry." Taya penetrated further into the woods and followed a small creek. Across the way, she spotted an overhang. "Grab some wood on your way."

She splashed across the water and filled her arms with fallen tree branches.

Tracy did the same, then sat and hugged her knees while Taya worked at starting a fire. "Won't someone see the smoke?"

"Maybe, but I doubt anyone will think anything about it. These mountains are full of cabins and hunters. I'm sure there is always smoke somewhere." At least she hoped so. She blew on the embers, then sat back to wait out the rain.

Soon, a curtain of water fell in front of the overhang effectively hiding them from anyone or anything that might pass—although, it would definitely surprise Taya to see anyone on two legs pass during the deluge. "We might as well stay the night here." The rain didn't look as if it would stop anytime soon.

"How will you know when we find a place to stay permanently?" Tracy rolled out her sleeping bag.

Taya doubted there would be anything permanent until the man leading the trafficking ring was behind bars. "I'll know it when I see it. I'd like to get to the top of the mountain I told you about before we start looking for a place."

"Is this mountain it?"

"Nope. That one is." She pointed through the rain toward the shadow of a much higher mountain. "Somewhere up there is our refuge." Taya unwrapped the bloodstained bandage from her upper left arm. It would leave a scar and most likely should've had stitches. But, there hadn't been time, and vanity wasn't one of her vices.

# Chapter Two

After a night of jumping at every sound, Taya struggled to her feet. The forest was full of sounds at night, and since she had no idea of the danger that would be coming for them, she felt as blind as a baby bat. Her gaze flicked to her sleeping niece. Her number-one priority. Finding those responsible for the trafficking ring came a close second. Achieving both seemed impossible.

"Time to get up, Tracy." Taya dug two apples from her pack. They'd need to stop for supplies soon. While her niece fought her way out of her sleeping bag, Taya pulled out the map where she'd marked the small mom-and-pop stores they'd pass. They'd reach one in less than a mile if they traveled via the road.

When the store came into view, Taya motioned for Tracy to stay out of sight. "I won't be gone long, but if someone is looking for us, they'll be looking for a woman and a girl. I have to go alone."

"Then at least buy more than one candy bar." Fear flickered in the girl's eyes. "And hurry back."

"I will." She cupped Tracy's cheek, then turned and crossed the road. Every nerve tingled as she opened the door, jerking at the sound of a bell jingling overhead.

"Good morning." A middle-aged woman smiled from behind the counter. "You must be hiking."

"Yes." Taya forced a smile and headed for the candy bars. First things first, after all. If sugar made her niece feel better, then sugar it would be.

She chose five, then grabbed a loaf of bread, peanut butter and jelly, some plastic silverware, a can opener, and assorted canned goods along with bottles of water. It was a lot to carry, but this was the last small store until they reached the top of Misty Mountain. Then, she'd have to figure out a way to get into town when they needed supplies. It wouldn't be a quick hike into the valley and back.

"That's a lot to carry, and it's fixin' to rain," the woman said. "Do you need some help?"

"No, thank you." Taya shoved most of the supplies into her backpack and hefted the case of bottled water onto her shoulder. "I don't have to carry it long. Thank you."

"Okay, if you're sure."

"I'm sure." Taya kept a smile on her face and rushed back to where she'd left Tracy, just as relieved as every other time to see her where she'd left her. She tossed her niece a candy bar. "Let's make it quick. We're almost to the top."

"Then what?"

"We find a place to hide out for a while." Once she found a way into town, she'd buy a used car under an assumed name, use a fake address, and pray it all worked to keep Tracy out of…whoever's hands.

At the top, she set down the case of water and her pack to stare over the valley. Fog drifted through the trees, and a fine mist settled above Taya's head. She'd never seen anything so peaceful in her life.

"Wow," Tracy said from behind her. "I didn't think views like this existed."

"Me either." It almost made her forget the danger coming.

They rested for a good half an hour before she pulled her niece to her feet. "Look for barely used paths. There should be a cabin down one of them."

"I hope so. I've never been this tired in my entire life."

Taya doubted that. Without having a place to stay, they hadn't yet discussed in any detail what her niece had gone through. That would come later when Tracy felt safe.

Spotting a path not too much further, Taya headed that way. Ten minutes later, they stood in front of a cabin that had definitely seen better days, but it did have a roof, four walls, intact windows, and a front door. It would suffice.

"Let's put our stuff on the porch and take a look around." She didn't want any close neighbors. At least not close enough to wonder why they'd just arrived. People could get nosy, which could lead to them being killed.

"Can we make it short? I'm tired of walking. Will we have internet? Wi-Fi?" Tracy peppered her with questions as they entered a clearing.

Two German shepherds raced toward them.

Taya spun around and gave her niece a shove. "Run!" She raised her rifle.

A piercing whistle split the air.

The dogs stopped.

A man stepped from the trees across the meadow.

~

Ryan Boyne stared at the woman and young girl his dogs had cornered. Since he hadn't seen a living person in over a week, not since he went to town anyway, it took a minute before he realized how terrified they must be. "Astro! Boris! Down, boys. Please, don't shoot." He jogged toward them, hands out. "Please."

The woman reluctantly lowered her weapon. "They were going to attack."

Ryan gripped both dogs' collars. "No, they would have only guarded you."

The young girl stretched out her hand, only to have the woman snatch it back. "Don't touch them."

"They really won't hurt her. It's okay." He glanced behind them. "You hiking? We don't get many people up this way." Which he liked. He'd rented his cabin because of the privacy and how secluded it was.

"Yes." Her features hardened.

"I'm Ryan Boyne." He let go of one of the dogs and held out his hand. When she didn't offer hers, he wiped his palm on his pants. "Well, maybe I'll see you around. Come on, boys." He flashed a smile he didn't feel. There was a story here—one he itched to find out more about. But first, he had a different story to finish.

As he headed away, the young girl complained about the absence of Wi-Fi. He stopped and turned. "You can log into mine if you're close enough. I don't have anything to write down the password, though. It's under BoyneCabin—one word, two capital letters."

"I can remember it." The girl smiled.

He'd rattled off the password before meeting the

harsh stare of the woman. She didn't like him talking to the girl. Very well. He'd let them be. "Have a good day." Ryan hadn't realized how lonely he'd become until seeing them. Sure, the dogs were company, and he'd rented the cabin for solitude to finish his book, but seeing people so close brought the loneliness home. Maybe he needed to go into town more.

What caused the woman to be so guarded? The girl, too, until he'd offered the Wi-Fi password. A flicker of interest had passed over her face when she tried to pet the dogs. He glanced over his shoulder.

The woman still watched, the rifle clutched in her hand. Why would hikers carry a rifle? The two also looked weary, so weary they could sleep for a week. No, these were not mere hikers. His curiosity grew.

"How would the two of you like to take a walk?"

The dogs' ears perked up.

"Let me grab a water bottle and something to eat before we head out." He wasn't sure what he'd find, but he suspected two campers hiding in the woods. Ryan always trusted his gut, and his gut told him the woman and girl were in trouble.

Did he really want to get involved? Yes. Whatever reason brought two gals up here might be just what he needed to overcome his writer's block. If he was wrong…well, it never hurt to go for a walk. Half an hour later, the dogs at his side, Ryan hiked in the direction the woman and girl had gone. He should hike more, especially with spring coming.

Cardinals and blue jays flitted through the evergreens. A squirrel chattered its displeasure at the interruption of a human and dogs. A rabbit bounded across their path. Both dogs gave chase, returning when

Ryan called their names. A hike might actually clear his mind enough so he could put fingers to the keyboard.

With every breeze, the cobwebs in his head seemed to clear. Every bird song put words in his head. Maybe, he'd have something to appease his publisher soon.

He sniffed. Someone had made a fire. Could it be the two he sought?

The two dogs stood at attention. They were close to someone. Ryan parted the foliage in front of him.

A dilapidated cabin rose above a yard of weeds. Smoke curled from a rock chimney. The young girl from earlier sat on a porch step, a cell phone in her hand.

A few seconds later, the woman came around the corner of the house and snatched the phone from the girl's hands. "Tracy, I've explained to you why this isn't a good idea." She held up the phone. "People can be found through social media."

"Aunt Taya, I'm making up a dummy profile. I'm not even using my own picture." Tracy crossed her arms. "Believe me, I know the danger better than anyone."

Ryan frowned. So, they were in some sort of trouble, and it appeared they were living in a cabin that could barely be called livable.

"Tracy…"

"What else am I supposed to do? That phone isn't linked to us in any way. I don't have any books to read—"

"We can buy you books."

"How? We don't have a car."

"I plan on buying one."

"By walking another three days down the mountain? No thank you." The girl scuffed her boot in the dirt. "I'm tired of walking."

Taya sat on the step beside her. "All we need is time, sweetie. This will end. I promise you."

"Can I have a dog? Someone to talk to?"

"Well, I…uh…Again that means going to town."

"So what?" Tracy bolted to her feet. "We're far enough away from those men. They'll never find us here. Never!" She stormed into the house.

Ryan had heard enough to chill his blood and make him uncomfortable at eavesdropping. He whistled for the dogs in order to alert the woman, then stepped from the trees, doing his best to look surprised to see her.

The expression on her face told him she didn't believe his ruse. "Are you following us?" She reached for the rifle leaning against the porch railing.

"No. I was walking the dogs and smelled smoke. I haven't smelled smoke in this direction before." He smiled and held up his hands. "No need to shoot. I'm merely an author out trying to clear his head."

"I know who you are." She rose slowly to her feet. "I've read your books."

Despite having a gun aimed at him, a rush of pleasure coursed through him. "I hope you liked them."

"What do you want, Mr. Boyne?"

"To give you and your daughter a ride into town. Tomorrow morning okay?"

"Why?"

"I thought you might need time to settle." He frowned.

"No, why do you want to help us?" Suspicion laced through her words.

"I'd like to think it's because I'm a nice guy. Can you lower that gun, please?" Astro growled beside him until Ryan slowly lowered a hand and laid it on the dog's head. "What do you say? Can I give you a ride?"

"Tomorrow. Eight a.m." She whipped around and hurried into the house.

# Chapter Three

Taya woke the next morning to see Tracy standing in front of the window. The slump of her shoulders told Taya everything she needed to know about the girl's mood. Defeat showed in every line of her body. "Sweetie?" She climbed from her sleeping bag and went to stand next to her niece. "Want to talk about it?"

"You've never asked."

"Asked what?"

Tracy gave her a red-eyed look. "About Amber."

Her best friend—the girl also allegedly taken from the coffee shop. Taya felt as if she was about to get confirmation. "Tell me now."

"Amber got sick and died about a week ago. She never was rescued." She launched herself into Taya's arms. "Amber died sick and afraid."

"I'm so sorry." Taya tightened the hug. "Are you ready to sit down and tell me everything you remember so I can write it down? The authorities can use any information we can give them." Her thoughts drifted to Mason. If anyone could have brought the trafficking ring to justice, it would have been him.

"Okay." Tracy's words were muffled against

Taya's shoulder. "Maybe getting it out of my head will help me move on."

Taya set her at the lopsided table in the corner and pulled her cell phone from her pack. She'd have to find a place in town to charge the phone. The battery had less than half a charge. "I'm going to record you, okay?"

Her niece nodded.

"Tell me what happened at the coffee shop."

"Amber and I were sitting at the table we always sat at. We sat there almost every day."

And someone knew that. "Go on."

"A really cute boy came up to us. Said he was new to town and asked if we could show him where kids our age hung out. Amber started flirting right away, but the guy had a look in his eye that made me nervous." She gave a shaky smile. "I must be as paranoid as you, Auntie."

"Nothing wrong with that."

She nodded. "Anyway, Amber said sure. We could show him the local burger joint. So, we picked up our drinks and followed him outside. As soon as we did, a van pulled up. Two men wearing masks jumped out and shoved us inside. It was that fast." She shuddered. "We didn't even have time to scream before they gagged us, put bags over our heads, and zip-tied our hands behind us. When we stopped, they led us to the cells you found us in."

"How many girls were there?"

She shrugged. "A lot. You saved them, so you know more than I do."

"You said they were…saving you for the highest bidder?"

"Yes. A doctor examined us, supposedly. Some of us were saved to get a higher price, others started…training." She bolted to her feet and fled outside.

The sound of vomiting brought Taya to her feet. She grabbed a water bottle and rushed outside. "Okay, we're done for today."

"No." Tracy held up a hand. "I'm good now."

"Drink." Taya shoved the bottle into her hand.

After she guzzled half the bottle, Tracy sat on the porch steps while Taya went inside to retrieve the phone. When she returned, she set the phone between them. "Tell me about the men. How many? What did they look like?"

"I don't know which ones took us other than the boy, and I never saw him again. The other men were older. Maybe thirty-something? I don't know. Old."

Taya bit her lip to keep from smiling. "My age or older?" She hated to believe that her turning thirty next month classified her as elderly.

"Older. Especially the one they called boss. His hair was graying. Not much but some. He had dark eyes. A big guy with lots of muscles."

"What about the others?"

"Some were around his age, some older, one or two younger." She scuffed her boot in the dirt. "They fed us twice a day. Oatmeal in the morning, a peanut butter and jelly sandwich in the afternoon. Three water bottles a day. It was like a prison."

Prisons fed better. Taya turned off the recorder on her phone. There wouldn't be any more information coming that would help. But, she did have confirmation that her niece could identify the leader. That would keep them in danger until the man was stopped.

"Oh, and there was a woman. Older. Mean. She would put the makeup on us and give us clothes to put on before our pictures were taken. All the men called her Ma."

Taya stared over the weed-grown clearing. A number of men and an older woman weren't a whole lot to go on. "Did they take you anywhere else, besides where I found you?"

"No, but some of the girls left. I never saw them again."

Taya's heart sank. They hadn't saved them all before they were sold. Spotting Ryan stepping from the woods, she pushed to her feet. "We're going to town. We'll get you some books, some better food, and charge my phone. Now listen. I don't want you getting into a conversation with this man. We don't know how much we can trust him."

"I doubt the men who took me would be all the way out here, Taya."

"We aren't taking any chances." Taya slipped her phone into her pocket. "I'll get the charger and some money. Don't move from this spot." She hurried to gather what she needed and rejoined her niece outside who had just finished telling the man their first names.

Ryan smiled. "My truck is parked just over there. The path to this cabin can't really be called a road in any sense of the word."

Taya nodded. "Lead the way." The gun she'd stuffed at the back of her jeans gave her comfort. If this man made a move toward her or Tracy, it would be his last.

~

The woman was as skittish as hot oil in a cast-iron skillet. Despite her unfriendliness, Ryan wanted to help. These two were in trouble and seemed like they could use a friend. Once in the driver's seat, he turned. "What's on the agenda?"

"The library, someplace to charge my phone, and a grocery store. Maybe a supermarket?"

"Sure. Langley has all those things. We can get a coffee while charging the phones, then hit the supermarket. On the way back to Misty Hollow, we can stop at the library. You'll have to use my card, though, since you're only visitors."

She made a noise in her throat and stared out the window. "I'll need to buy a vehicle."

"The garage here in town might have one cheap." A car, huh? Maybe they planned on staying for a while. Ryan could take them to the garage first and let them run the errands on their own, but curiosity won out. He wanted to know what haunted this woman and what put the fear in the girl's eyes. The only time the girl had relaxed was with his dogs. "Want to stop at the pound? Your daughter mentioned wanting a dog."

"I'm her niece."

Taya shot her a sharp look. "We don't need anything to take care of."

"Please? I don't have any other form of entertainment." Tracy bumped her aunt with her shoulder. "Besides, a dog is a good warning system."

"Stop talking." Taya narrowed her eyes.

"Well, it is." The girl crossed her arms and slouched in the seat.

So, they needed a warning system. The mystery around them widened.

"It'll be too difficult to take a dog with us when we move on."

"No, it won't. We're buying a car."

Taya sighed and returned her attention back to the window. "Fine, but I pick out the animal. Nothing fluffy."

Ryan had a strong feeling the girl got most of what she wanted. He grinned and turned on to the interstate to head for Langley.

Taya's constant furtive glances behind them started to set Ryan's nerves on edge. "Are you expecting someone?"

"No."

"My aunt is always…nervous. She spent too much time in the military. Special forces. It made her hard." Tracy picked at a loose thread on her sweater.

"I said to stop talking." Taya exhaled heavily.

PTSD maybe? Ryan trained his attention on the road in front of them. If the woman didn't want to talk, he wouldn't force her to. But, with no one talking, the twenty-minute drive would seem much longer.

As soon as they entered the Langley city limits, Tracy started clamoring about the dog. "Come on. We can take it into the store with us. No one will care."

Taya closed her eyes as if she had a headache. "Pick your battles," she muttered. "Fine, Mr. Boyne. The dog pound first."

Once at the pound, Taya marched straight for the door that said large breeds. Barking immediately assailed them. She peered in each cage and read each sign on the cage door before finally stopping.

Ryan read the sign. "Betty. Seven-year-old female. Former military and service dog."

"I'd like to meet this one, please," she told the attendant.

"Oh, good. Betty is scheduled to be euthanized in a few days. No one seems to want the older dogs." The attendant opened the door and clipped a leash on the dog's collar. "Follow me."

She led them to a fenced-in, grassy area and removed the leash. "I'll be back in fifteen minutes. Enjoy. She's a real sweetie."

"I don't want a sweetie. I want a guard dog." Taya tilted her head.

The woman grinned. "I'm sorry, sir. Please step outside the fence."

"For what?" Ryan's eyes widened. He was pretty sure he wouldn't like what was coming.

"Protect the girl."

The dog lunged for Ryan, barking as if she wanted to eat his face.

"It's okay, girl. Watch him."

The dog sat, keeping her dark eyes fixed on Ryan.

Taya smiled. "What else can she do?"

"Pretty much whatever you tell her. Once she knows she belongs to you, she'll die for you."

"You know this dog." Ryan slowly reentered the yard.

"She belonged to my brother. I wanted to keep her, but I live in an apartment. That wouldn't be fair." She rubbed the dog's ears. "Breaks my heart. Please take her." She glanced from Ryan to Taya. "She comes with a service vest, although you'll have to register her under your name."

"We'll take her." Taya's smile widened.

Tracy dropped to her knees, wrapped her arms

around the dog, and sobbed.

~

"No sign of them, boss." Moore stepped back as Boss stood from behind his desk.

"Keep looking. They can't have disappeared. You're one of the few the girl hasn't seen. I want them brought to me." Boss had plans for Trapp, and the girl was still worth a lot of money. Once she saw what he could do to her, she'd cooperate easily enough.

"Can I take a chopper up? Try and locate her vehicle?"

Boss waved a dismissive hand. "Whatever it takes. Search the whole state and the neighboring one. Check every small town in every valley and mountain. While you're at it, check every state surrounding this God-forsaken Oklahoma. Just bring them to me." He'd give his right arm to be back in California at the beach. But, he needed the large amount of money trafficking these girls brought in. It might take a while to find the girl who escaped, but he would find her. Of that he was certain.

Maybe he'd retire overseas. Buy a villa. Have a handful of beauties waiting on him. He returned to his seat.

Once he stopped Trapp and the girl from ruining everything, he'd have all he'd ever dreamed of—everything his time in the US military didn't bring him. Money and comfort. He grinned. Yep. Money and comfort. He could feel them, smell them. Victory was within his grasp.

Maybe Moore couldn't find them on his own. He picked up the phone and ordered the only other two the girl couldn't identify to join the search. "Do whatever it takes, but I want the girl unspoiled. Try to bring the woman alive, but if you can't, she's expendable."

He'd try and convince her to join him. To see the monetary benefit. If not, she was easy to dispose of.

# Chapter Four

Taya tore her gaze away from her crying niece and glanced at Ryan. Shock and confusion flickered across his face. When he met her gaze, she looked away. The less he knew, the better for him. "Come on, sweetie. We've lots to do today."

"Can Betty be my dog?" Tracy kept her arms around the dog's neck.

"Absolutely." A dog with this training would die before letting anyone harm Tracy. Taya and the dog had a lot in common.

She ushered the dog and girl to the front where she paid the adoption fee and put on the dog's service halter. Betty looked up at her with wise dark eyes that also showed compassion. "We've seen a lot, girl, haven't we?" She ruffled the dog's ears and avoided the still curious gaze of Ryan. Once she had her own vehicle, she'd have to make sure the man didn't come visiting anymore.

Ryan drove them to the supermarket where Taya ordered Tracy to stay close and to keep a tight hold of Betty's leash. Taya grabbed a cart and headed for the clothing. She had no idea how long they'd be in hiding and she'd brought the bare minimum.

As she filled the cart with warm clothes, even adding a battery-operated lantern and a couple of flashlights before heading down the sports aisle, the guy kept silent. Eyes as dark as the dogs and every bit as wise followed Taya's every move. His intense study of her sent goosebumps prickling her skin. What was he thinking?

When her cart brimmed to the top, Ryan grabbed another and took the full one from her. She filled the second with things for the dog and food for her and Tracy. She'd buy ice for the cooler in Misty Hollow. "There. This ought to do us for a while."

"Looks like you plan on staying." Ryan arched a brow. "Can I help you pay for this?"

"No, thank you. I've got it." She stepped into a short cashier line. "Now I won't need to come back into town for a week or two. I prefer buying in bulk."

"So, to the bookstore, then to the garage in Misty Hollow?"

She nodded. "If you don't mind."

"Of course not. I offered, didn't I?"

When she glanced around them, lingering on anyone who seemed curious, he did the same. Taya would have to be more careful about keeping a watchful eye out, or he'd become suspicious, if he wasn't already.

He didn't speak again until they were on their way back to Misty Hollow, the back of his truck full of food, clothes, and books. Halfway there, he pulled off to the side of the road and turned in his seat to face her. "What's going on?"

"What do you mean?" She tried to look innocent but knew she failed. She'd never had a good poker face.

Tracy and Betty stared from the back seat.

"Don't act like you don't know what I'm talking about. You've been on edge since the minute my dogs ran up on you in that meadow. You're constantly looking over your shoulder, expecting someone to be there." He frowned. "I've made a career out of studying people, Taya. If you're mixed up in something dangerous, I have a right to know. Am I in danger?"

"No. You're simply giving us a ride. Once I have my own vehicle, we'll keep our distance." She shot Tracy a warning look.

Her niece wrinkled her nose and flounced back.

His eyes flashed. "So, you are mixed up in something."

"I didn't say that."

"You didn't have to."

"Can we please go home?"

"Home?" Both his brows rose to his hairline. "I happen to know that cabin you're in has been abandoned for months. Maybe a year. Did you contact the owners, or are you squatting? If you plan on staying a while, spring break is almost over, and school starts back on Monday."

"That is none of your business."

"You're a horrible liar." He yanked the wheel and stomped on the gas, rocketing them back onto the interstate.

Again, silence prevailed until they pulled into the Misty Hollow garage. Sitting to the left of the building were an SUV and two sedans.

Taya marched to the SUV, noted the sticker price of eight thousand, and talked the guy down to five. She dug the money from her pack, noticed how low her funds were getting, but she refused to be dissuaded. If they found they needed more money, she'd find a way to get some. Title in hand, she returned to Ryan's truck.

"I'll transfer our things, and you can leave. Thank you for your help today." She grabbed several bags from the truck bed.

He shoved his door open. "I'll help."

"Again, thank you." She really did owe the man but had no idea how to repay him. It was best if she kept her distance. Keeping him out of her trouble would be the best form of thanks. She closed the back of her SUV and thrust out her hand. "Thanks."

He returned the shake with a solemn nod. "Whatever it is, Taya, I'm here if you need help. With anything. Even if it's simply calling the sheriff's department."

Heavens no. The last thing she needed was the involvement of local law enforcement. She forced a smile and climbed into the driver's seat.

Ryan pulled out of the lot behind her, obviously intending on following them home.

Her blood ran cold halfway up the mountain. She'd made a rookie mistake when purchasing the SUV. She might have paid with cash, but she hadn't used an alias on the title. Lord, don't let that be the biggest mistake of her niece's life.

~

Ryan followed the SUV until it pulled off on what might have once been a road toward the abandoned cabin. Shaking his head, he headed to his rental. What was Taya running from?

He'd picked up a few things in Langley himself and carried them into his cabin. Astro and Boris waited, tails thumping, for the treat they knew would be coming their way.

"Here you go." He tossed them both a piece of dog bacon and put his groceries away. When he'd finished, he eyed the laptop on the kitchen table. There was a story with Taya and her niece, but he didn't know enough yet. Not enough to start writing, anyway. He needed to know more about her. It would help if he knew her last name, but Taya wasn't a common name. And, she had said she had been in the military.

Time to do some research. He turned on his laptop and started digging. It didn't take long to find her military photo. Taya Trapp, seven years with the last two in special forces. Then, she'd simply quit. Why?

More digging uncovered the fact she'd had a sister Tania, now deceased. Tracy must be her daughter. After an hour, he gave up, not finding anything more as to why they were hiding on top of Misty Mountain in a ramshackle cabin.

Could it be connected to something she'd worked on while in the military? She'd been a marine. Maybe something in the Middle East? If so, why drag a teenage girl into the midst of whatever danger she found herself in?

He drummed his fingers on the table. His gut told him whatever she was hiding from was big. Huge, even.

Ryan moved from the table to the back door and let the dogs out. If he did find himself in trouble because of spending the day with Taya, he had the best warning system available. Not much got past Astro and Boris. He kept a handgun in his nightstand and ammo in a box on the top shelf of his closet. It might be time to keep the gun loaded.

He shook off the thought. No sense inventing trouble without proof. Maybe Taya was simply a woman who preferred to be left alone. No. She was running from something.

Grabbing his cell phone from the table, he stepped outside and headed down the path toward her cabin. He didn't know why he felt compelled to keep a watchful eye on her and the girl, but he did. Sure, the dog she'd adopted could probably do a better job than he could, but his curiosity about what Taya hid from wouldn't let him go.

Someday, she'd need him. For what, he had no idea, but he intended to be there when she did. When her cabin came into view, he motioned for the dogs to sit quietly at his side.

The girl sat on the porch step, Betty at her side. Every few minutes, Taya stepped to the doorway and glanced outside. She was definitely expecting something or someone.

He watched for a few more minutes before turning and going back home.

~

The Boss listened as Moore rattled on about coming up empty for yet another day. "I'm aware it will take a while. Widen the search."

"Yes, Boss."

Taya was a smart, tough woman, but she wasn't invincible. She'd make a mistake eventually, and he'd be there waiting for her. Oh, yes. He knew Taya almost as well as she knew herself.

He stood and stared out the large window overlooking pastureland. A neighbor had several head of cattle grazing there but left those in his house alone.

A good thing. Nosy neighbors didn't live long around him.

Killing wasn't something that bothered him—not after all the killing he'd done in his career. A career that had prepared him for his current occupation. He grinned. Time to find a new place to stash fresh cargo. Then, he'd upload photos to the dark web, and the money would start pouring in. They had some recouping to do after Taya rescued the latest batch. Those who had paid for a girl were getting impatient. He pressed a button on the phone on his desk. "Get me Jason."

A few minutes later, a good-looking college-aged boy entered the room. "Boss?"

"I need you out there drumming up fresh produce. Don't hit the same town as before, though. Mix it up. One or two girls here, one or two there. By the time you score, I'll have a place to put them. Until then, the barn will do. I want them as innocent as you can find without having to wait too long. Time is money."

"Yes, sir." Jason backed from the room.

Boss returned his attention outside. Spring approached quickly, warming the air. In the distance, storm clouds gathered. So far, he had yet to experience a tornado and hoped it would stay that way. But, if not, he hoped one hit before he had a barnful of merchandise. He didn't need the walls blown down and girls escaping to give him away. Not again.

No one got the best of The Boss. No one.

# Chapter Five

Ryan hadn't spoken to Taya in over a week. That didn't mean he didn't check on her from the protection of the trees once or twice a day. Even then, he still had no idea what made her so afraid.

Once, he'd arrived to check on her only to see her vehicle gone. Just when he started to worry, she arrived with her niece, Betty, and several grocery bags. Another time she moved from the SUV to her makeshift home with an armful of books, most likely from the library, which meant she'd given an address. Did the old hunter's cabin even have one?

Today, Taya split firewood like a lumberjack, her strong arms glistening with perspiration as she raised the axe and let it fall with a thunk. She might be beautiful with a head of mahogany-colored hair and eyes the color of a spring meadow, but she definitely wasn't soft. In fact she was unlike any of the women he'd ever met.

His gaze fell on the rifle propped against the house. She rarely let the weapon more than an arm's reach away. When her dog stepped onto the porch and glanced toward where he hid, he melted back into the trees and headed home feeling every bit the stalker.

As he cut across the meadow in back of his rental, he sniffed the air. Smoke. He glanced around for the dogs. Not seeing or hearing them, he strolled toward a small rise.

Not too far in the distance, a plume of smoke rose. Hunters or campers, most likely. While he rarely saw anyone this high up, he did run across the occasional camper. Since it wasn't hunting season, he hoped he wouldn't find poachers that he would legally have to turn in.

The solitude was what had drawn him to the top of Misty Mountain. That and the view as the sun came up and mist filled the valley below. Now, with Taya and these new, yet unidentified people, that very privacy was threatened. At this rate, he'd never finish his book.

Keeping his rear in the chair hadn't worked. His mind went blank every time he stared at the screen. Why had he lost his muse? His publisher emailed once a week asking for an update. At the rate Ryan was going, he'd be asked to pay back his advance.

He whistled for the dogs and headed toward the smoke rising above the trees and realized he was procrastinating again. The dogs caught up to him. Together, the three of them approached the area where Ryan could now hear voices.

He motioned for the dogs to stay and be quiet before peering through the foliage. Two men, both with backpacks and semi-automatic rifles, huddled around a fire despite the warming temperature. They were definitely not hunters. Not with those type of weapons.

"I'm telling you she's around here somewhere. The Boss said she bought a vehicle." One of them held a hot dog on a stick over the fire.

"Yeah, well, I don't like nature. This traipsing around, living out of a sleeping bag, is for the animals. We'd better find her and the girl quick, or I'm taking off."

"Sure, you will. The Boss will hunt you down like the cowardly dog you are." The man holding the stick cursed as his hot dog fell into the fire.

Ryan moved back, inch-by-inch, taking extra care not to step on a twig or make too loud of a rustle. Those men could only be talking about Taya and Tracy. Now that he'd stumbled across her reason for hiding, he needed to warn her that those looking for her were on the mountain.

As he rushed to her cabin, his mind spun with ways he could help her—ways he could keep her safe. He wrote about these types of situations. Yes, he could come up with something, couldn't he? Something she'd agree to?

Astro and Boris sniffed the area as Ryan made haste back to Taya's. If she said she didn't want his help, if she said she'd run, what would he do? He'd have no choice but to let her go. Maybe he could convince her to talk to Sheriff Westbrook. He seemed like a reasonable man.

Taya was still chopping wood when he stepped into the opening. One look at his face and she stuck the axe in a block of wood. "What?"

"Huh? There appears to be a couple of men looking for you on behalf of someone called The Boss." He swallowed past the boulder in his throat as she paled to the color of a cloud in an azure sky.

"How do you know this?"

"I saw smoke and followed it. Two men were

sitting around a campfire. I overheard them talking about a woman and a child. I want to help you."

She reached for her rifle. "There's nothing you can do."

"Sure, there is. They're looking for a woman and a girl, not a family. You can pretend to be my wife and Tracy my daughter." It would work if they didn't know what she looked like.

She laughed. "You spend too much time in a fictional world, Ryan."

"At least talk to the sheriff. He might know what to do. The sheriff's ex-FBI. He'll have connections."

She faced him, her smile gone. "No one can. Not yet, anyway. Tracy and I will move on."

"For how long?" He reached out to stop her, pulling back at the harshness in her eyes. "You can't run forever. Let me help you."

"You have no idea who you're dealing with. It's too dangerous. Why would you put your life in danger for a stranger?"

He shrugged. "I'm a nice guy."

"You're a bored author."

Some of his niceness drifted away. "That's an unfair assumption." Despite the truth.

She tilted her head. "I know you've been checking up on us, Ryan. Whenever I hear about authors, I know how many hours they spend writing. I've yet to see you stay home long enough."

"Again, that's unfair. You have no idea what I do in my cabin." His face flushed. "Fine. Forget I said anything. I'll leave you alone and pray I don't stumble across your dead body someday." He turned to leave.

"I'm sorry. Don't storm away."

He turned back.

"I do appreciate your concern. Really. But, there isn't anything you can do. I do promise to speak to the sheriff. Today. Whatever he tells me will determine my next step. The last thing I want is to bring danger to this town." She pivoted, climbed the steps, and disappeared into the house.

~

"Are we really going to the sheriff?" Tracy buckled her seatbelt. "I thought you said the police can't help us."

"Maybe I was wrong. Running isn't going to keep us alive. The Boss will find us. We need to be ready for him when he does." She reached over and took Tracy's hand. "I won't let him take you again."

"You mean you'll try not to allow that to happen." Tracy stared out the window. "If we're going to come out of hiding, can we move somewhere with electricity?"

"We'll see." Taya chuckled and backed away from the house. She really hoped she was making the right choice. Not wanting to continue running was a sure thing. Wanting to draw The Boss out into the open was another sure thing. Hopefully, neither would get them killed.

"Why won't you let Ryan help us? He seems like a nice guy." Tracy cut her a quick glance.

"I don't want to involve anyone that can be killed." She couldn't handle being responsible for the death of an innocent person.

"I dream of that cell every night. The cry of the other girls. The last time I saw Amber." Tracy's words broke off. "I want this to stop."

"I'm trying." She gave her niece's hand another squeeze. "We'll find you a counselor. Someone who can help you through this."

"Betty is all I need." She stared out the window. "What happened is private. Now, the sheriff will know. It's only a matter of time before Ryan knows."

"Maybe not. I'll hold him off for as long as I can, but he definitely suspects something." *Nosy writer.*

It didn't make her mad that he wanted to help. It had been a long time since anyone had worried about Taya. She hadn't been lying about not wanting to put him in danger, though. What could a crime author do to keep her safe? Write her a happy ending? Any happy ending she'd get would come by her own devices.

She parked in front of the red brick building that housed the sheriff's department, then stashed her handgun in the glove compartment. "Keep Betty on her leash, okay?"

"Sure." Tracy shoved her door open and clicked the leash on the dog's halter. "Are you going to leave me in the waiting room?"

"Yes. Does that bother you?"

"A little. Bad people go in there, Taya." Tears welled in her eyes.

"You have Betty. If someone bothers you, all you have to do is yell. I'll come running. I'm pretty sure the sheriff's office is the safest place to be." Unless the sheriff was crooked, which she prayed he wasn't. Even FBI agents could be bought. She'd even brought down a couple in her time.

Inside, the receptionist told them to sit, not batting an eye at the sight of Betty. Taya led Tracy to a line of hard plastic chairs and sat.

A couple of minutes later, the receptionist spoke. "You can go on back. First door on the right past the bull pen."

"Remember. All you have to do is yell." Taya cupped Tracy's cheek, then headed in the direction the woman had directed her.

A woman and a male deputy glanced up, then returned their attention back to their computers. Another male deputy stepped from a room, a cup of coffee in his hand. He offered it to her.

"No, thanks." Taya knocked on the door of the sheriff's office, then entered when summoned.

"Have a seat, ma'am." A handsome man folded his hands on his desktop. "I'm Sheriff Westbrook. How can I help you?"

"Where to start..." She took a deep breath and gave her name and credentials.

His eyes widened. "I bet you have quite the story to tell, Miss Trapp."

"Yes, sir." She went on to tell him everything she knew from the time Tracy was abducted from the coffee shop.

"Now, the two of you are hiding on Misty Mountain, and Author Ryan Boyne asked you to be his pretend wife in order to keep you safe. Do I have that correct?"

"That about sums it up."

He kept a sharp gaze on her. "What do you feel is your next move, ma'am?"

"I don't want to run. I want this trafficking ring stopped."

"Do you know where they're based?"

"We found the girls in Oklahoma." She described

where they'd been held. "I made a mistake using my real name when I purchased the SUV. Can you give me and my niece new identities until The Boss is stopped?"

"Witness Protection?"

"Except we stay here in Misty Hollow."

"You wouldn't be the first," he mumbled. "Fine, Miss Trapp. I can get you new identities. I can even fix the title to your vehicle as if you sold it, but I think it would be best if you sold it and purchased something new under your new name." His gaze speared hers. "There is safety in numbers. Mr. Boyne is often a consultant for law enforcement. He's that knowledgeable. I believe he can help keep you and your niece safe."

She narrowed her eyes. "Are you saying I should take him up on his offer of a pretend family?"

"Yes. He is very well-known. A few newspaper articles, some online news about his marriage, and you might have the best cover you can find. Change your and your niece's hair color as well."

Taya chewed the inside of her cheek. "That puts Ryan in danger."

"It does." He made no apology.

"Then why?"

"Because I've learned since becoming sheriff of this town that folks are going to help whether you want them to or not. With you being under the same roof, you're also protecting our Good Samaritan. With his brain and your experience, it sounds like the most viable option to me." He asked a few questions about her vehicle. "My wife has something similar. She'll buy yours and you buy hers under your new name. If someone digs deep enough, they might figure it out, but it would be a waste of time."

"How long until I'm someone else?"

"Half an hour. I have contacts. Taya is too original. Who would you like to be?"

She thought for a minute. "Anita Fuller…Boyne. My niece will be Amber." There'd be no turning back.

# Chapter Six

Ryan opened his front door to see the sheriff accompanied by a blond Taya and a red-haired Tracy. Behind them, Betty sat, tail stirring up dust. Something had happened. He stepped back, holding the door wide.

"Meet your wife, Anita, and your daughter Amber." Sheriff Westbrook handed him a navy-blue folder. "I suggest you make the cabin she was in look as if no one had been there in years."

He glanced at the folder. "Witness Protection?"

"Yep. For now. Since you offered to take them in, and I don't have the manpower to spare, we're taking you up on that offer." The sheriff flashed a grin. "I suggest you take some photos for your social media. Your readers are going to go nuts when they hear."

Ryan's eyes clashed with Taya's, uh, Anita's. Heck. He'd have to be careful what he called her in public. "Okay. We'll make up a story of how we met, etc., and try not to get her face or Tracy's full-on in a photo."

The sheriff nodded at Taya. "I told you he was smart. Have a good day, folks. I'll have my deputies watch for newcomers. Give the office a yell if you need us."

After seeing the sheriff out, Ryan turned to his silent "wife and daughter." "Let's go clean out your cabin. You'll need to put your things in the master bedroom, even if you plan on sleeping with Tracy in the guestroom. If we have any uninvited visitors, we want them to think we share a bed." He headed for the front door, then glanced over his shoulder. "Well, are you coming?"

Tracy glanced at Taya who nodded. "Yes."

"The hair looks nice on you." He smiled, liking the way the modern bob framed her face.

"Hmmph." She brushed past him, headed for his car. "Do you really want three dogs in your luxury SUV?"

"We'll take your…Jeep?"

"I had to sell and buy something different under my new name." She opened the back door for Tracy and the dogs. "Scoot them all into the very back. This is ridiculous." She slammed the door.

"What is? Keeping you safe?"

"Driving around with three dogs. Betty is sufficient."

"My dogs would pout all day." He laughed and climbed into the front passenger seat. "I haven't really spent much time in town. That's something else we'll have to do. We'll need to be seen out and about a bit. Hiding will raise suspicions and people in small towns talk."

"As little as possible, please. I doubt changing hair color will fool The Boss if he looks close enough." She turned the key in the ignition and drove to the cabin they'd stayed in.

He'd be glad to have them out from under the

sagging roof. Especially with the expected rain for the upcoming week. "While you pack your things, I'll take care of covering your tracks." He headed for the woods.

Ryan broke off a large branch from a pine tree, then gathered other small bits of debris to scatter across the porch. He'd use the branch as a broom to muff any sign of footprints. There wasn't a whole lot he could do about the clean floor inside the cabin. Hopefully, any nosy lookers would see the yard and think no one had been there. Only time could put another layer of dust on the floor.

"How do you know all…this?" Taya waved her arm where he'd scattered leaves and twigs.

"Research. We writers are always researching. While we might not have actual experience, we'll have read about it or interviewed someone." He wiped his dusty hands on his jeans. "If it can be imagined, we've thought about it."

"Writing sounds fun." Tracy glanced around the porch. "You sure made a mess in a short amount of time."

"That's the idea." Taya patted Betty's head. "Where are the other two dogs?"

"Always sniffing around unless I order them to stay." He put two fingers to his lips and let out a piercing whistle. "They'll be here. Are we done?"

"I think so."

"Good." He grinned. "We need to take some photos."

She rolled her eyes and sighed. "Remember not to get our faces."

"I'll remember."

He told her to pull over to an outlook. He put an

arm around her, backs to Tracy who had his cell phone, and waited until the girl said she was done. "Now, a selfie. Taya, you gaze up at me like you love me. Big smile." He stretched his arm as far as it would go. "Tracy, you look off in the distance, okay?" He counted to ten, then grinned before the flash went off. "That's the one I'll use to announce our quick wedding."

"Oh, goody."

"Do you have any family that might wonder…if they were to see a photo? Friends?"

She shook her head. "I've been too busy for friends, and since I grew up in the foster system, any family is long gone."

That would make things marginally easier. Keeping a smile on his face, he stared down the road where the two men he'd spotted around the campfire strolled toward them. "Tracy, in the car, please. Pretend you're sleeping, hair over your face. Take Betty with you. Taya…"

"I'll be on my phone in the passenger seat." She climbed into the SUV.

With Astro on one side of him and Boris on the other, Ryan greeted the hikers. "Nice day, gentlemen."

"Couldn't ask for better." The one who had lost his hotdog glanced at the Jeep, then the dogs. "Y'all out for an afternoon drive?"

"Sure are." Ryan widened his grin. "Just got married in Langley, and now we're on our way home." He lowered his voice and leaned forward. "Got the little lady knocked up. You know how it is."

"Good luck, buddy." The men laughed and kept walking.

~

Knocked up? Taya would strangle him with her bare hands. She glared at him as he climbed into the driver's seat. "Really?"

"I had to think of something fast. That's something those two goons would've thought was funny. They didn't spare the Jeep a second glance."

The man had actually done very well. Maybe he was as smart as the sheriff thought. Ryan might've made good in the special forces. Still, she couldn't allow herself to get too close to him, to trust him too much. The only person she could trust one-hundred percent was herself.

Back at his cabin, she unpacked the few items she possessed in the master closet, then joined Tracy in the room they'd actually share. Thankfully, the room possessed a queen-sized bed because the dog usually slept curled up next to Tracy.

"This is much better." Tracy folded a pair of jeans. "Wi-Fi, TV…a refrigerator! Definitely a step up."

"Just don't forget to call him Dad."

"Since I don't remember my dad, and my mom didn't talk about him before she died, that shouldn't be a problem. I don't have anything to compare Ryan with." She closed the drawer with a bang. "Now what?"

"We try to stay alive long enough to find The Boss."

Tracy plopped onto the bed. "I'd rather not ever see him again."

Taya knelt in front of her and took the girl's hands in her own. "You don't have to. All you need to do is point him out to me, and I'll take care of the rest. Okay? I won't let him hurt you."

"Okay." Tracy sighed. "Let's go see what lies

Ryan is cooking up so we all stay on the same page." She stood and held out her hand.

Hand in hand, they joined Ryan at the kitchen table.

"Let's write our story." He turned his laptop so she could see the screen. "I uploaded the two photos. Posted about how we met on my last book-signing tour in Florida. A whirlwind courtship we kept private until signing the marriage license."

"Why keep it a secret?" Taya crossed her arms. "I don't care that you said so, but I need to know why."

"We met in college. You got pregnant with our daughter, Amber, but only recently revealed to me that I was a father. We fell back in love and got married." He tilted his head and smiled. "I think this is getting rid of my writer's block."

"Glad to help." She chewed on the inside of her cheek. "Okay. That story works. I studied art in college but dropped out when I got pregnant."

"I studied journalism, which is the truth, and switched colleges—also true."

At least one of them wouldn't have a hard time keeping most of the facts straight. She glanced at Tracy. "Why the service dog?"

It took a second for the glimmer showing she understood to shine in her niece's eyes. Tracy thought for a minute, idly scratching behind Betty's ears. "I'm chronically shy. That way, if we do meet people, I won't have to say anything and can keep my head down." She spoke barely above a whisper. "It won't be hard to pretend that at all."

Taya's eyes stung, and she stepped outside to keep Ryan from seeing the emotions welling. Her niece was one of the bravest, strongest people Taya had ever met, but day by day, the deep wounds were starting to show. The Boss needed to be put away so Tracy could obtain the help she'd need to fully heal.

She turned and watched through the back window as Ryan leaned against the kitchen counter and said something to Tracy that made her smile. A surprised, genuine smile. Loneliness assailed Taya. She was being silly, since she was definitely not alone. Not with a man, a teen, and three dogs, yet seeing how easy Tracy could trust Ryan after the kidnapping left Taya feeling as if she was missing something.

Ryan caught her watching and tilted his head for her to join them.

She shook her head and turned away, choosing instead to let the peace of the view wash over her. Trees stretched as far as she could see. A slight rise let her know they weren't exactly at the top of the mountain. An eagle soared overhead, floating in a sea of light blue.

A few minutes later, Ryan carried paper plates and sodas to the patio table. "Frozen pizza okay? We might need to make a run into town for food. A single man doesn't eat much."

"Don't go to any extra trouble for us."

"We could eat supper at the diner. Let people see the new family in town, then pick up some things." He glanced into the house. "Amber, you want to start a grocery list? Amber?"

"Oh. Sure."

Taya heard the sound of drawers opening and closing. "You think someone might be close enough to hear?"

"Not really, but it isn't a chance we should take. I've already seen those two men looking for you twice. Odds are high we will again."

"I agree. If we aren't within the safety of these four walls, it's Anita and Amber." She stared into eyes the color of dark coffee. "Thank you. This is going above and beyond."

"Hey." He shrugged, his eyes twinkling. "Part of it is definitely selfish. I needed a way to break through the writer's block. This whole thing has my mind spinning with plot ideas. It's I who should thank you."

She gave a sardonic chuckle. "Let's see if you feel the same way if you come face-to-face with The Boss." When *he* came face-to-face with The Boss.

# Chapter Seven

**The next morning**, minus Astro and Boris, they climbed into the JJeep and headed to town. As she drove, Taya did her best to psyche herself to the fact she'd have to pretend to be madly in love with the man beside her. She'd never been in love before. How did someone act?

"I haven't been around long to make many acquaintances." Ryan cut her a glance. "Most of the people will know me from my books. They might give you a curious glance, but they'll mostly want an autograph or for me to sign a book."

"I'll keep my head down and pretend I don't like the attention." Which wouldn't be a lie.

"The diner has outdoor tables if you'd be more comfortable outside."

"I would." Maybe. Being outside left them exposed to anyone driving by. Eating inside, gave them little space to escape. "Especially with the dog."

"What about leaving her in the car?"

"No." Tracy piped up from the back seat. "She goes wherever I do."

Taya shrugged. "Outside it is." The spring morning didn't require much more than a light jacket. She could sit with her back to the road, along with Tracy. Anyone looking for them wouldn't expect a family. Ryan's crazy idea might just work.

They'd no sooner sat at an outside table when a smiling server greeted them. "You can bring service dogs inside." She handed them each a menu.

"We're fine out here." Taya forced a smile. "It's a beautiful morning."

"It sure is. I'll be back to take your orders. What can I bring y'all to drink?"

Taya and Ryan ordered coffee while Tracy asked for an orange juice. So far so good. No one paid them any attention. No one sat at the other outside tables. Other than a quick glance their way from those at the inside tables near the windows, people pretty much ignored them…uh-oh. A middle-aged woman burst through the diner door and rushed their way.

"Mr. Boyne! I'm one of your biggest fans." She clasped her hands across her heart. "If I'd known you were here in town, I'd have brought all my copies of your books. Oh, wait until I tell my book club."

Taya's blood chilled. This was not a good idea. Too many people would be flocking around Ryan for them to be safe.

"I heard you got married," the woman gushed on. "Such a lovely bride, too. Welcome to Misty Hollow. I promise to have an armload of books the next time I see you."

"When you do, I'll be glad to sign them for you." Ryan shot Taya an apologetic look.

Thankfully, the server returned, and the fan went back inside the diner. "Have you decided?"

"I'll have the biscuits and chocolate gravy." Taya

handed her the menu.

"Me, too." Tracy grinned. "Chocolate for breakfast!"

Ryan laughed and ordered the breakfast special of three eggs, bacon, hashbrowns, and toast. "Can you bring us another side of bacon for the dog?"

"Absolutely." The server smiled at Betty and headed to turn in their order.

"I'm surprised you're sitting with your back to the road." Ryan arched a brow and added cream and sugar to his coffee.

"Believe me, my skin is prickling. I don't want to chance those two men driving by and recognizing me or…Amber." She dumped two sugars into her cup. "They've already met you, heard about your nuptials…it just seemed best to sit facing away from curious people."

"Then I promise to be your eyes." He reached over and put a hand over hers.

She jerked back.

"Sorry. I, uh…" Ryan sighed and turned his attention to his coffee.

"No, I'm sorry. Anyone watching would think it odd that I pulled away. I'm not used to being touched."

Tracy glared at her. "You're being an actor. Act."

A loud sigh escaped. "You're right. I promise to do better." She crossed her heart.

Ryan kept the conversation on normal things such as their grocery list, what they wanted to watch on TV that evening—all things Taya suspected married couples talked about—until their server returned with their food. He eyed her chocolate gravy. "I should've ordered a side of that."

"Where are you going to put the food you ordered?" No way he could possibly eat it all.

"Right here." He rubbed his stomach.

"Enjoy." The server smiled. "I'll be back to check on you. Oh, and the woman in the window paid for your meal."

Taya stared at the fan who had visited their table. The woman wagged her fingers. Despite her innocent demeanor, frigid shivers skipped up Taya's spine. She forced a smile, then ducked her head as Ryan waved at the woman. "Give her our thanks."

"Yes, sir." The server rushed away.

"That was nice."

"Yeah." Taya cut into a biscuit dripping with butter and chocolate gravy. Not even her favorite splurge of a breakfast could erase her twanging nerves.

They should've run upon finding out about the men searching for them in town. Was it because of the title on the SUV? Did The Boss have the ability to dig through DMV records? If so, the trafficking ring was bigger than she'd thought. Staying in Misty Hollow would bring the ring here. Girls would disappear, and there wouldn't be anything she could do to stop it.

Taya reached over and gripped Tracy's hand. She'd focus on keeping her niece safe and leave the rest to the authorities.

~

A myriad of emotions flickered across Taya's face. Fear, regret, tension…none of which he could erase for her. "We'll shop for groceries quickly so we can hurry home."

She nodded. "Yes, we've made our appearance. I'd rather not come to town again unless we absolutely have to.”

“I need a library card.” Tracy stuffed the last of her biscuit in her mouth. “I’m going through the books we bought real fast.”

“That won’t take long,” Ryan promised. “I doubt we’ll run into any bad guys in the library.”

“If that’s where young girls hang out, they will be thee.” Taya crumbled her napkin and tossed it on her plate. She dug in her purse for some money and set it under her plate. “I’m ready.”

“I’ll leave the tip.” He widened his eyes. “We’re talking trafficking, aren’t we?”

“Yes. The tip is already taken care of.” She stood. “Please. Let’s hurry so we can get back fast.” She cast a quick glance up and down the street before ushering Tracy back to the Jeep.

Ryan followed her gaze. While cars were parked up and down the street in front of various stores, only a few people strolled the sidewalks, and not one of them looked toward the diner.

Even though the library was within walking distance, they decided to drive. He took up the rear as Tracy and Taya shoved open the double doors.

“Make it quick.” Taya glanced at Ryan. “We can apply for the card while she browses the shelves.”

He nodded and moved to the front desk. Less than five minutes later, he had a library card. The librarian hadn’t asked how long he planned on staying in town, and he didn’t offer the information. Despite his trying to make light of the circumstances, Taya’s constant being on guard kept him glancing over his shoulder, too—something he’d never done before despite his search history on the internet.

"I found five." Tracy approached the desk, her arms full. "This ought to keep me busy for a week."

Back in the JJeep, Ryan glanced at Tracy in the rearview mirror, then at Taya. "What about school? Shouldn't she be homeschooled or something? How long has she been out?" Had Tracy been trafficked? That was a question he needed the answer to, but he would wait until the girl wasn't within hearing distance.

At the grocery store, he let Tracy help him fill the cart, then insisted on paying for the food. "New hubby, remember?" He jerked his head toward a woman watching.

Taya grinned. "It'll take some getting used to, sweetheart. Of course, I'm happy to let you take over paying for everything." She started putting their purchases on the conveyor belt.

"Newlyweds." Ryan smiled at the woman who nodded.

The ride back up the mountain was silent. Ryan stopped the JJeep, then asked Tracy to take Betty into the house. When she did, he cut the engine and turned to Taya. "The men looking for you belong to a trafficking ring, don't they? How does this concern you and Tracy?"

She scratched the brow above her right eye and sighed. "I was part of a team that rescued Tracy and a group of other girls from a ring in Oklahoma."

"Special forces team?"

"Unofficially. Private team." She pressed her lips together. "I joined them after getting out of the service when Tracy was abducted. I'm sure you know part of that. You did research me, right?"

"Absolutely." He crossed his arms. "How long was

Tracy with them?"

"Six months." She held up a hand as he started to speak again. "She wasn't touched. Not in that way, but she saw things. Her best friend, Amber, died in there. The two were abducted from outside a local coffee shop."

"Which is why you don't let her out of your sight."

"That's right. I did that once. I…" she cleared her throat. "I didn't have custody of her yet the month before she disappeared. My job took me away too much. After my sister died, I wanted to finish my time in the service, but God had other plans, I guess. I quit the day after Tracy went missing and called an old comrade of mine who had started working for a private contractor. Once we had enough information, we went in. My friend didn't make it out."

"That isn't your fault."

She shrugged. "Maybe, but I feel as if it is. If I hadn't been there for Tracy, none of this would have happened."

"You don't know that." He pulled the keys from the ignition and slipped them into his pocket. Remembering they weren't his keys, he pulled them back out and handed them to Taya.

"Still glad we're here?" She narrowed her eyes.

"Now that I know exactly what we're dealing with, I can help. It makes sense to keep Tracy out of the public eye. Can she identify the man who took her?"

"Yes, and The Boss."

Ryan's mouth dried to cotton. "You think he'll come for her?"

"Yes. And you and I are expendable." She shoved her door open. "Now, you know."

He sure did, and the knowing seized his heart in a grip of ice. He might have written a book where the bad guy ran a trafficking ring, but research and living it were two very opposite things.

Now that he knew exactly what he was dealing with, he'd make sure to keep his gun loaded and handy. He'd make sure the dogs were always close to the house. No more roaming the mountainside. They had no better security system than the three dogs.

Taya slammed the passenger side door to the Jeep and stared at him through the window with eyes the color of an emerald and just as hard and cold. He considered telling her to run, then rejected the idea.

Sheriff Westbrook thought it best she stay and help draw out The Boss. Taya wasn't a woman unaccustomed to danger. She knew what she had gotten herself into and planned to see it to its end.

Which meant, so did Ryan. Would he have made the same offer of a place to stay if he'd known the whole story? Probably. When someone needed his help, most of the time he offered his help without gaining all the facts.

He could only hope he hadn't made an offer that would cost him his life.

# Chapter Eight

**The Boss listened** to what seemed like a repeat report of the day before and the day before that. "She couldn't just disappear with a kid! That town isn't that big. They're on the mountain somewhere." Did he always have to do things himself? "There's a campground up there. Book all the sites. If someone is staying on one, run them off, bribe them—whatever it takes. Tell the attendant it's a family reunion. Be quick about it. I'm on my way." He cursed and hung up, wishing he had an old-fashioned receiver to slam down.

The Boss called someone else and barked orders for enough campers to house the ring, then marched to his room to pack. It wasn't the first time he'd had to live on assignment. He doubted it would be his last. He tossed some things into a duffel bag, then checked his guns and ammo. He'd need to be careful that Trapp didn't spot him. If she did, the gig was up. She'd sound the alarm and ruin everything. He cursed again.

Camping was not his favorite thing to do, even in a camper. He needed to start taking girls again. Maybe a few boys. Where was he supposed to stash them and train them at a campground? He shook his head and made another call for something that would suffice as a place of operations. "I don't care what you find, just make it work."

Duffel bag in one hand, weapon bag in the other, he headed to the garage and stashed both items in the back. The Boss didn't have to check whether his orders would be followed. Not following them would result in unpleasant consequences for the one who failed. He climbed into the driver's seat of his black SUV and drove to the undisclosed meeting place. The others knew without having to be told to gather here.

By nightfall, the dirt lot was filled with campers and fifth wheels. The Boss strolled among them until finding the one he liked. "This one." Inside, a person would barely know it was a camper. Up-to-date appliances, separate bedroom, and full bath and shower. He would be comfortable. "Let's head out. Form a convoy." He gestured forward, then climbed back into his vehicle and led the way.

As he drove, his mind whirled with the possibilities of a new location, albeit a temporary one. It might not be wise to take teens from Misty Hollow, but there were plenty of outlying areas and nearby towns. Finding Trapp and the kid wouldn't be easy with his workload, but he'd find a way to make locating them a priority.

They made it to the campground at sunset. The Boss strolled up to the attendant's "box," pulled his handgun, and shot the grinning man between the eyes before the man could register what was about to happen. He snapped his fingers at a middle-aged man who worked for him. "Dispose of the body. You're the new camp attendant. That camper is your home for now. You're this man's cousin and are taking over while he's on vacation. Make sure there isn't a woman waiting for him in the camper. If there is, dispose of her as well." He climbed back into his vehicle and drove to a site in the center of the campground.

The sound of another gunshot let him know the attendant had found someone waiting for him in his camper. The Boss sighed.

Law enforcement would show soon. You couldn't drive a long line of campers and RVs through town without attracting attention. Unfortunately, there hadn't been another way to reach the campground.

He wasn't wrong. An hour after they showed up at the campground, a sheriff's car pulled through the gate, spoke with the man in the attendant's box, and then headed The Boss's way. He pasted on a smile, before grabbing a rag from the back of his truck and pretended to wipe his hands after setting up his temporary home.

"Howdy." He approached the man getting out of the car.

"Howdy yourself." The sheriff stood a few feet from him. "All you folks together?"

"Yes, sir. College fraternity, some relatives, lifelong friends…heard the fishing was good around these parts." He thrust out his hand. "Bill Lincoln." Not his real name, but it would do.

"No women on this trip?" His shrewd gaze roamed the campground.

"No, sir. Just the men's yearly thing. We chose Misty Hollow this year."

"How long are y'all staying, Bill?"

"At least a week, maybe longer. Depends on the fishing." He kept the smile plastered on his face. "You can't beat the scenery." He glanced toward the lake.

"No, you can't. Welcome to Misty Hollow." He glanced at the attendant's box.

"Something wrong?"

"No, I'm just not used to ole Hank taking a vacation." He nodded. "Enjoy your stay." He slid back in his car and drove away.

Bill narrowed his eyes. The sheriff was no dummy. He might cause some problems. If he did, the good ole boy would have an unfortunate accident. No one came between The Boss and what he wanted.

~

Taya watched all three dogs race to be the one to fetch the ball her niece tossed. A normal scene, a happy scene, but it wouldn't last. Evil was coming. It was close. She felt it to her core. Taya raised a coffee mug to her lips and scanned the area behind the house. Anyone watching from the trees wouldn't assume anything more than a family lived there. Three big dogs should dissuade anyone from coming close uninvited. So why the tense knot between her shoulders?

"You okay?" Ryan joined her on the deck and leaned against the railing.

"Today I am."

"That's all we can ask for, isn't it? In a situation like this, it's one day at a time."

"Hmm." She set her cup on the railing. "It's just that I'm not used to waiting. I'm usually the one who goes after the bad guy rather than letting him come to me."

"Which keeps Tracy safer?"

"Letting The Boss come to us." She sighed. "I just want our lives back."

"What is that?" He arched a brow. "Your normal

life?"

"I don't know. It was special forces. Then, six months of searching for Tracy. I don't know what my life will be after this." It pained her to know she had no idea what the future held.

"It'll be whatever you make it." He smiled and glanced to where her niece played with the dogs. "She'll be a part of it, whatever you decide. Because of you, Tracy and other girls will have a future. Do that with your life. Keep saving kids being trafficked. You have the experience a lot of people don't."

She tilted her head up at him. "You're a smart man, Ryan Boyne. I can't think of anything I'd like more than to save more kids." There was bound to be some reliable groups out there working on stopping trafficking that could use her skills. She could spend her time now researching those. "I need to purchase a laptop."

"Okay. You can use my account. I'll go log you in." He took her cup into the house.

She called Tracy to come in, then followed Ryan to the kitchen table. After researching several models, she decided on a laptop that would suit her needs. "Where do I have it shipped?"

"The post office in town. I have a PO box there." He leaned over her shoulder, filling her senses with a musky cologne. "Here." He tapped the screen. "Looks like you'll have it in two days. Until then, you can use mine."

She glanced up, bringing her face uncomfortably close to his. She cleared her throat and looked away. "Didn't you start writing again?"

He chuckled and stepped back. "I don't write

twenty-four hours a day, Taya. I'm a morning writer. There's plenty of time to share."

"Can I use your laptop?" Tracy grabbed a glass from the cupboard, then filled it with tea from the refrigerator. "I miss social media."

"Absolutely not."

She frowned. "I have a new name. I'll use a fake photo. What's the big deal? I'm not stupid enough to be taken again."

"We aren't taking any chances." Taya's tone should've told her niece to stop.

Tracy dug in her heels. "Stop treating me like a child. I'm no longer the stupid little girl you knew. I've seen things!" She whipped around and stormed back outside.

"I don't want you outside alone." Taya started to stand.

"Stay." Ryan put a hand on her shoulder. "Let me try to talk to her as an impartial party."

"Are you impartial?" She narrowed her eyes.

"Absolutely not. But, that's our secret." He smiled and followed Tracy.

Taya stood at the window and strained to hear through the thick walls of the log cabin. She could see why Ryan liked the place so much. Even the simple construction offered privacy. At that moment, she wouldn't have minded cheaper materials used for the walls. All she could make out were muffled voices and very little of those.

~

"What do you want?" Tracy glared. "Did my aunt send you out here?"

"No." He leaned his back against the railing in

order to see her face. "I came of my own accord. What's going on? I know you aren't stupid enough not to see the dangers of getting on social media."

"Of course, I'm not. But, that's where predators lurk. One is bound to contact me. We can set a trap."

Lord, help them. The girl thought she'd be helping them catch The Boss. "I don't think that's a good idea."

"Of course, you don't. You're like Taya." She smirked. "Too old to go out and grab what needs grabbing."

He silently counted to ten to keep from saying something he shouldn't. "You aren't being fair to your aunt. Tracy, you have no idea what your disappearance did to her. What she went through to find you."

"Neither do you." She faced him, defiance in every line of her face. "We just met you, *Dad*. You really don't have a say in what we do."

"Yes, I do." He clenched his teeth. "This is my house. I've put my life on the line for the two of you. Don't mess this up by acting like a brat. Now, get in the house."

She opened her mouth to argue, then snapped it shut and stormed inside.

Ryan shook his head. He'd heard teenagers could be difficult, but wow. After what the girl had gone through, he wanted to be empathetic, but he wouldn't let her mess up Taya's plans on bringing down The Boss by putting herself in more danger. He glanced around the kitchen when he entered the house.

"That doesn't look as if it went well." Taya closed his laptop.

"It didn't." He poured them both a glass of tea, added ice, then sat across from her. "She thinks she can lure The Boss out of hiding by putting herself on social media."

"That scares me spitless." She guzzled her tea. "Isn't she aware of the danger?"

"Yes. She also pointed out that I am not her real father, thus not able to tell her what to do. I told her to stop being a brat and to get in the house. Is she in her room?"

"She went that way." Taya shot a look toward the hall. "I heard a door slam. Where's Betty?"

Ryan's blood chilled. He bolted to his feet and down the hall. "Tracy?" He jiggled the locked doorknob. "Open the door, please."

"Break it down." Tracy backed up and raised her leg to kick.

"Hold on, Rambo." He reached up and took the piece of metal from the doorjamb and unlocked the door.

The room sat empty.

The curtains fluttered over the open window.

"I'll get my gun." Taya darted back to the kitchen.

Ryan retrieved his weapon from his room and called to the dogs. They'd find the girl quickly. They had to. Before someone else did.

# Chapter Nine

Heart in her throat, Taya followed close on Ryan's heels as he followed the dogs into the woods. Her only consolation was the fact Tracy had taken Betty with her.

What if she ran into those two men? Would they recognize her? Her heart beat faster. Of all the things Taya had faced during her career, this frightened her the most. She couldn't fail her niece.

Ryan glanced over his shoulder. "We'll find her. The dogs know this mountain. She can't have traveled far."

Taya nodded, wanting to believe him. Instead, dread filled her.

One of the dogs ahead of them barked.

Ryan bolted ahead, Taya right behind.

They burst through some brush to find Tracy sitting on the bank of a creek, her arm around Betty and tear stains on her cheeks. Taya dropped to her knees and wrapped her niece in a hug.

"You scared me to death. Why did you run away?"

"Because you won't let me help. I'm not a child." She stiffened in Taya's arms.

"But...you are." She searched her niece's face.

"I'm fifteen. That is not a child." She shook her head. "The Boss wants me. I can identify him. Let me help you stop him before he takes someone else."

Taya met Ryan's concerned gaze over the girl's head.

He shrugged and glanced across the creek. "Someone is coming. Get her out of here."

"Come on…Amber. Let's go home." Taya gripped Tracy's hand and pulled her to her feet. "Come, Betty." As the two men who kept showing up whenever they were in the woods stepped into sight, Taya and Tracy melted into the shadows on the other side.

"Howdy again!" One of them raised a hand in greeting.

"Hello." Ryan moved to block their view of the fleeing Taya and Tracy.

"No need for them to leave. We're only sightseeing."

Taya ducked, putting her finger to her lips.

Tracy nodded, eyes wide.

"My daughter ran off. The wife is taking her home to ground her. You know how teenagers are."

"I'm not married or a father myself. Neither is Larry here, but we can imagine." The man laughed. "Name's Darrel."

"Ryan Boyne."

Darrel frowned. "Why does that name sound familiar?"

"I'm a writer." Ryan took a deep breath. "Nice to see you again. I'd best go help the wife."

Taya kept her gaze on the two men as Ryan turned and stepped into the trees where she hid with Tracy. He jerked his head down the trail, then whistled for the dogs to follow.

His unease pricked her nerves. She had the feeling Ryan didn't think the men as innocent as they seemed. Neither did she. Why did they always show up…unless they were watching the cabin? "Have you seen any sign of those men close to the cabin?" She asked once they were well out of hearing.

"Not that I know of. The dogs would let us know if anyone came around."

"Trouble is getting closer. I feel it."

He glanced back. "So, do I."

"Not to nag or anything," Tracy said, "but this is why you should let me draw him out."

Taya glared. "The answer is and will always be a firm no."

Tracy set her jaw and marched ahead of them, back straight.

With a sigh, Taya shook her head. She wasn't very good at being a mother figure to a teenage girl who had experienced something a lot of adults would crumble under.

"She'll be okay." Ryan took her hand.

Taya stiffened, then relaxed. The simple gesture comforted her as Ryan most likely intended it to. Nothing romantic about it. "I hope so."

"How is the research going as to how to help other girls?"

"Slow. What I need is to find a reliable group that can use my help. The problem with that is…I can't leave Tracy, so any help I do has to be from behind a computer. I'm not sure that will be good for much."

"Anything is better than nothing." He nodded toward the house. "Sheriff is here."

Taya's heart fell. His visit could be a good thing, but her gut said otherwise.

~

Ryan released Taya's hand and offered his to the sheriff. "What brings you out here?'

Sheriff Westbrook returned the handshake. "Nothing good, I'm afraid.

"Exactly what I thought." Taya crossed her arms. "Tracy, go inside, please."

"I don't think so." She plopped onto a deck chair. "This probably involves me."

The sheriff shrugged. "Not directly." He took a deep breath. "We've received a report from Langley PD about a missing sixteen-year-old. She left school yesterday and never made it home."

"Are you sure she was abducted?" Ryan glanced to where Tracy sat, eyes wide, straining to hear the sheriff's words.

"Everyone we've spoken to said it wasn't like her not to let her parents or at least a friend know where she was going." He removed his hat and raked a hand through his hair. "I'm letting you know so you can keep a lookout. Keep Tracy close."

"Can I talk to you away from—" he jerked his head toward the girl.

"Sure. Walk with me to my car."

Ryan fell into step as the sheriff returned to his vehicle. "Tracy has been difficult. She insists on using social media to draw out the predators. Said she's the only one who can identify The Boss."

"True, but she's too young. We don't even use informants under the age of sixteen, and then only when we're desperate." He slapped his hat back on his head.

"Anyone new in town?"

"A lot of folks. The campground is full of a men's group. Said they're here fishing."

Ryan frowned. "Do you believe them?"

"No reason not to at this point, but I'm definitely keeping an eye on them. Since Tracy is so determined to help, I advise you not to mention the fishermen to her." He went on to tell him how long the men planned on staying.

"I agree. If she finds out, she'll head over there to check them out. Thanks for the heads-up." Ryan stepped back as the man climbed into his car and backed away, before turning to drive down the mountain.

"What did you need to talk to him about?"

He glanced back. "Where's Tracy?"

"In the house pouting."

"He said the campground is full of fishermen. Someone booked the whole place for a minimum of a week. I've never heard of anyone booking an entire campsite before."

She shrugged. "I have. Family reunions and such. Maybe we can find time to sneak away and check them out."

The curtains in the front window fluttered. "Getting away from little Miss Nosy is going to be the hard part."

Taya gripped his arm. "We can't let her find out. What if it is The Boss? He'll take her. I doubt I'd find her again. I should take her away from here."

"And run for the rest of your life?" He pulled free and put his hands on her shoulders. "Taya, listen to me. I understand your fear, but you are a strong warrior.

You can keep her safe and bring down those responsible. I'm here to help you."

"You're a writer."

He raised his brows. "The sheriff trusts me."

"I'm sorry. I do too." She leaned her forehead against his chest. "I'm so scared, Ryan."

"And, I'm willing to guess that you've never relied on anyone's help before."

"Not a civilian."

"Maybe it's time. Who would expect a writer to be involved?" He held her at arm's length and grinned.

"Don't writers stick their noses in places they shouldn't and call it research?" She returned his smile.

"I plead the fifth." He put his arm around her shoulders. "Let's go eat." He tried to ease some of her burden, but not even his joking could take away the prickle running down his spine.

Misty Hollow might be a mountain town, but it wasn't impenetrable. He'd read the newspapers over the last couple of years. The town's very seclusion often worked against it.

He paused before entering the house and stared at the thick woods. Lots of places to hide, spy, and sneak up on someone. Thank God for the dogs. He patted both their heads before following Taya inside. It wouldn't be easy for anyone with evil intentions to get close to the house.

"Secrets?" Tracy arched a brow. "I thought we were a team."

"We're two adults and a child who won't stop gnawing on a particular bone." Taya went to the kitchen, calling back that she was making sandwiches.

"So, you going to lecture me again?" Tracy

glowered.

"Nope." Ryan locked the front door, then locked the back before returning to the front room. "Tracy, you are not an adult yet, but you're also not stupid. You have a very important job to do."

"Which is?"

"Staying safe and not driving your aunt insane."

~

Bill smiled at the sight of the three portable buildings. Two for "training" and one to hold the new girls. At that moment, the one Jason had taken was tied up in one of the bathroom stalls. Bill had yet to meet her—something he intended to remedy as soon as he finished supervising the placement of the portables.

"Sir?" Jason stepped to his side. "Permission to leave? I've another target. Langley has a dance studio, and I know when the teenage girls dance. There's a recital tonight. I'm bound to find one of them alone."

"Good job. Remember…not too many from one town. You might have to travel a bit." Bill clapped the young man on the shoulder. "Keep it up, and I might have to promote you to trainer."

"I'd sure like that. Beats the grunt work I do now." He grinned and turned to jog to his vehicle, a cliché white panel van with the word florist on the side.

All of the men wanted to be trainers, but only a few had the privilege. Above all, they had to be one hundred percent trustworthy. Jason was proving he could be trusted.

Bill turned and marched to the brick building housing the women's bathroom and shower. He could hear the crying before he opened the door. That wouldn't do at all. What if a hiker wandered by?

Yanking open the door, he called for the girl to shut up. The crying changed to a whimper. He moved to the last stall and stood over a petite red-haired girl, big blue frightened eyes over a gag, and a dusting of freckles across her nose. She couldn't be more than fourteen.

"My, my." He hunkered down in front of her and ran the back of his hand down her soft face. "You are a pretty thing. You're going to bring me a lot of money. Are you pure, or have you been with a boy? Nod if you haven't been with a boy."

The girl shivered and gave a quick nod.

He grinned. There would be no training for her. This one had to be kept unsullied. "Don't worry. No one will bother you. Not until you're sold anyway." He pushed to his feet. "I'll fetch Mary to clean you up and dress you so we can take your picture. Won't that be fun?"

The only woman in camp, Mary was a middle-aged woman who preferred to dress and act like a man. But, she did know how to dress a girl properly and apply makeup. That's all Bill cared about.

More tears spilled down the girl's cheeks.

"No fighting when Mary gets here, you hear me? We don't want to mar that lovely skin of yours or addict you to drugs. You behave, and everything will be just fine." Another pat to her cheek and he left the building. Jason sure did know how to pick the girls. Except, it was too slow. He needed another hunter prowling the streets.

The question was who? Most of his men were too old to attract young girls and he didn't have time to find another young man without a conscience. He sure didn't want to go out there himself. Thirty-five was too old.

Maybe he'd forget the grooming and use the old-fashioned snatch and grab. He had plenty of men qualified to do that. Plans made, he headed to find a few hunters. He'd lost a lot of time and money when Taya rescued those girls.

# Chapter Ten

A week had passed with no sign of The Boss. Taya sat on a deck chair, drummed her fingers on the wooden arm, and stared into the trees as the three dogs nosed around the property.

She'd filled her time by communicating with a couple of groups that specialized in tracking down traffickers and waited to hear whether one, or both, of them could use her expertise. She hoped so. The idleness of waiting for something to happen was about to drive her mad.

"I made coffee." Ryan handed her a cup before sitting in the chair next to her. "Tracy is inside working on an assignment. Good idea enrolling her in an online school."

"Hopefully, she can catch up during this spring and over the summer." She took a sip of the coffee made just the way she liked it. Lots of vanilla cream. "Thanks. How do you always remember the little things? The details?"

"Writer, remember?" His eyes twinkled over the rim of his cup.

"Can Tracy sneak out?" Taya ducked her head so he wouldn't see how much she enjoyed the look in those azure eyes when they rested on her. She couldn't get involved with a man now or probably never. Her line of work didn't leave much room for romance.

"If she tries, she won't get far. I installed alarms on the doors and windows." He chuckled. "The piercing sound should scare her back inside."

"Brilliantly devious." She turned her attention back to the woods. "You have a great view. Have you ever thought about buying this place?"

"It's not for sale."

"Everything is for sale if the price is right."

"Hey." He set his cup down. "How about we forget about all…*this* for a while. Let's grab lunch at the diner and drive around looking at the sights? The lake is gorgeous, and there's a hiking trail."

It didn't take long for her to make a decision. Not only did she need a break, but it would do Tracy good to get away for a while. "That sounds great."

An hour later, bringing only Betty with them, they headed down the mountain for lunch. They sat at one of the outside tables again.

Taya surveyed the parking lot. "This place does a good business. It's packed."

"It did well even before the group at the campground. Lucy's is a staple for Misty Hollow." He glanced at his menu. "The special is chicken fried steak."

"Too heavy for lunch." She chose a BLT and chips. "Could I have cream cheese instead of mayo?" She handed her menu to the server.

"Absolutely." The girl smiled and left to turn in their orders, promising to bring a hamburger patty for Betty.

While they waited, Tracy seemed to study every

face at the adjoining tables and turned to stare at every vehicle that pulled up to the diner. She'd narrow her eyes, peer hard, then shake her head and mumble, "Not him."

"Stop looking for The Boss or you'll…conjure him up." Taya frowned.

"I'm not a witch, Taya. I thought you wanted him to come so we could end this."

"I do."

"Well, then—" She took a big gulp of her soda. "Make up your mind."

How did anyone survive teenagers? Yes, Taya wanted The Boss to show himself, but she didn't want him to pose any danger to her niece. Unfortunately, she couldn't have both. Tracy would be in danger when the man arrived, and Taya wasn't sure she could keep her safe. Taya didn't know what she'd do if she lost her again.

As if he could read her mind, Ryan reached across the table and put his hand over hers. "We're all in this together. Whatever happens."

She nodded and forced a smile. "I know."

They finished eating and piled back into her Jeep. She stared out the window as they drove toward the lake.

"The hiking trail goes clear around the lake," Ryan said. "On one end is the campground. At the other end is the dam which you can walk across. It's a pretty hike."

"I could definitely use the exercise." She'd been idle for so long she felt as if she were getting out of shape. "Is there a gym in town?"

"No, but Langley has one."

She glanced at Tracy who shook her head. "I'm not going to the gym."

Well, she'd have to find another way to stay in shape because she wasn't leaving the girl behind. Hiking would be a good start.

A short way past the campground, Ryan turned into a gravel parking lot. On one side of them shimmered the lake. On the other was the campground which resembled a beehive of men, campers, and portable buildings. The group must be planning on something grand.

A few rowboats and kayaks sat on the shore of the lake waiting for someone to take them onto the water. "Let's go kayaking." Taya shot Ryan a questioning look. "We can do that and hike. It's been a long time since I've kayaked."

"What about Betty?" Tracy crossed her arms.

"She can ride in front of me."

"Sounds like fun." Ryan grabbed a life jacket and tossed it to Tracy. "Put that on." He pulled a backpack from the Jeep. "Water bottles and snacks."

Taya took one and stuck it under a stretchy piece of cord. She could swim well, but if she did need the life-saving device, it would be within arm's reach. "Come, Betty."

She pushed the kayak into the water, splashed in after it, then sat and motioned for the dog. Betty didn't need coaxing. She jumped on, making the kayak rock before she settled down in front of Taya.

Once the other two were backing from shore, Taya did the same. She glanced up as a man moved from a camper to the restroom.

Mason? No, it couldn't be. She'd seen his body

dragged away. Taya blinked a few times, and the man was gone. Yep, she was losing her mind. She gazed across the lake, thinking of the man she thought resembled Mason. Someday, when things settled down, she'd have to process her feelings over losing such a close friend.

~

They rowed close to the shoreline until they reached the opposite side. Ryan's kayak bumped the shore. He climbed out and pulled the kayak onto the sand. "Want to see the view from the dam?"

"Yes." Tracy copied him, then shed her life jacket.

It surprised him that she hadn't argued about wearing the device since he and Taya only had theirs in the kayaks. "We can stop for some snacks."

"I can definitely use some water." Taya glanced toward the campground.

"Something wrong?"

"No. I saw someone who reminded me of a friend who's gone now." She gave her kayak another tug.

"Are you sure it wasn't him?"

"I saw him die, Ryan." She stared him down. "Not even an award-winning author can bring someone back from the dead except on paper."

He held up his hands. "Sorry."

"No, I'm the one who should apologize. None of this is your fault. My friend, as well as I, know the risks of our job."

"Ready to hike to the dam?" He tilted his head, wishing he could take the pain from her eyes.

"Yes." She gave a mock bow. "Please, kind sir, show us the way."

He hitched the backpack higher on his shoulders and headed down the path. The warm early afternoon sun warmed his shoulders. Other than the thuds of their feet on the dirt path and the birds twittering in the trees, no other sound reached them until they hiked close enough to hear the water spilling over the dam. He couldn't think of a better way to give Taya and Tracy a respite from their troubles.

The thundering of the water would drown out any noise from Tracy's time with the traffickers. Make it impossible for Taya to focus on anything other than the sheer power under their feet.

They stood near the safety of the railing. No one spoke until Ryan told them to turn around. "Now, look the other way."

"Wow." Taya smiled.

Behind them power, in front of them the serenity and peace of a placid lake kissed by the sun. She glanced up at him, her eyes shimmering. "Thank you."

He smiled. "You're welcome." He dug granola bars, water bottles, and a dog treat from his pack and handed them around. "There is a lot of beauty around Misty Hollow. Despite the roughness of the last couple of years, it's still a place most people feel safe living in."

"What about you? Will you move on when this over?" Taya wadded the wrapper from her granola bar into a ball and slipped it into the pocket of her jeans.

"I'm not sure yet, but I think I might take your advice and make an offer on the house I'm renting. I'm getting my muse back." He grinned. "Why take a chance on losing it again?"

She laughed. "I think you were simply bored until

we showed up."

"That is also true." He had been bored and lonely despite the two dogs. He knew their "marriage" was only a farce, but once Taya and Tracy left, loneliness would again be waiting. Well, he wouldn't dwell on that. The only future he needed to focus on was keeping his fake wife and daughter safe from evil. Despite all the research he'd done, he had no law enforcement background, no special ops training, nothing that qualified him other than the sheriff's belief he could. Taya was far more qualified than Ryan.

"Can we move on?" Tracy broke through his thoughts.

"Sure." He moved across the top of the dam until they were back on the path. "Do we walk the rest of the way around or paddle back?"

Taya glanced at the sky. "Paddle. Those storm clouds are coming up fast."

He'd hate to be caught on the water if it started lightning. "Let's hurry."

They picked up the pace. It started to drizzle as they set off across the water. Ryan scanned the shoreline for somewhere to hole up if the weather worsened, wishing they'd opted to hike despite the rain.

A clap of thunder sounded overhead.

Tracy screamed.

Betty yelped.

"Paddle faster." Taya dug her paddle into the water and skimmed across the surface.

"To the right." Ryan pointed to a brick building. "We can take shelter there."

She nodded to let him know she'd heard and veered in that direction.

By the time they pulled to shore, the clouds had opened. Rain fell in a deluge.

Ryan waved them on and sprinted for the protection of the building, holding the door open for the others.

"That's the men's room." Tracy headed the other way.

"It doesn't matter." Ryan groaned and followed them to the other side.

From under the awning of a camper, a man stood, watching them. Ryan lifted a hand in greeting, then closed the door behind them. "It won't be very comfortable for a long period of time, but it's dry." He set his pack on a metal bench and removed his shirt, then pressed the hand dryer and held the soaked piece of clothing under the hot air, continuing to press until the shirt had mostly dried. "Next."

"I'm good." Taya sat on the metal bench and toed off her shoes. "I'd rather not strip down, if you don't mind." She jerked her head toward Tracy who did everything but look at Ryan.

Idiot. He quickly donned his shirt. He hadn't thought about how seeing a man without his shirt on might affect the girl after her experience. "Sorry. I didn't think about anything other than getting dry."

"It's okay," Tracy said softly. "I can't be a frightened mouse for the rest of my life. I'm bound to see some things that bother me."

He sat next to her on the floor. "You're one of the bravest people I've ever met."

She smirked and cut him a sideways glance. "You haven't met many people then."

# Chapter Eleven

The rain had slowed from a torrent to a drizzle. Taya stepped back from the door. "We can make it to the car now if we cut through the campground."

"Sounds good to me." Ryan grabbed the backpack.

Taya stepped outside, located the clearest route to the parking lot near the lake, and took off in a sprint between the campsites. A man lifted a hand in greeting as they dashed past him. She leaped over a puddle only to land ankle deep in another. Her shoes squished as she ran.

Behind her sounded the heavier thuds of Ryan and the occasional gasp and groan from Tracy. The only one who seemed to be enjoying their run through the rain was the dog who loped alongside of them, tongue hanging out, purposely splashing through every puddle they came across.

By the time they reached the Jeep, as wet as when they'd entered the bathroom, they broke out laughing. Taya swiped hair from her face. "Good thing I don't have cloth seats. We're nothing but a bunch of drowned rats."

"I was going to take y'all to supper, but I think I'll order pizza." Ryan opened her door for her, then the back passenger door for Tracy and the dog.

"Sounds great. A hot shower, comfy clothes, pizza, and good movie." Taya climbed in and shut her door. Across the lake, the sun began a slow peek between the clouds. "Looks like it's clearing up."

"Right after ruining our outing." He turned the key in the ignition.

"No, it was a great day." She reached over and rested her hand on his arm. "Thank you. We did need this."

"You're welcome." He returned her smile and drove up the mountain.

Thankfully, he had two showers. Taya took the one in the master bedroom while Tracy rushed to the second one. The hot water washed away the chill of the early spring rain. When she'd finished, Taya felt like a new woman.

She pulled on a pair of black yoga pants and a tee shirt before moving to the living room. "Your turn."

"Great. Pizza is ordered. Money is on the table if the delivery comes before I'm finished." He peeled off his shirt on the way.

Taya took a moment to admire the muscles of his strong back. It had taken all her willpower not to ogle him in the campground restroom. The man was definitely built. Asking him to put his shirt on had been as much for her benefit as Tracy's. It had been a long time since Taya found herself attracted to a man, but now was definitely not the time.

Taya sat at the table and opened her laptop which had arrived the day before. She had several emails, one from one of the groups she hoped to help. Her blood chilled as she read.

A third girl had disappeared from Langley, and the group wanted to know whether Taya could take a look around town, do some investigating, find out if the trafficking group she'd broken up had moved to Arkansas. She straightened in her chair.

Could she? What would she do with Tracy? Yes, Taya wanted to help in any way she could, but leaving her niece alone while she did so was out of the question.

She glanced down the hall toward the master bedroom. Would Ryan keep an eye on her? He had no right to keep Taya from doing whatever she wanted, but that wouldn't stop him from trying to stop her.

Taya studied the photos of the missing girls. All around the age of fourteen. All blond. All blue eyes. Just like Tracy. She closed the laptop and moved to the back kitchen window. Gathering clouds cast the woods into deep shadow and promised another storm.

Everything in her wanted to help stop this ring. Everything in her wanted to protect Tracy at all costs. She felt as mentally stretched as a rubber band and as useless as a hunting dog who couldn't smell.

The water in both showers shut off. She shook her head at how long of a shower Tracy had taken. Well, Ryan could speak to her if he was concerned about the water usage. Tracy rarely listened to Taya anymore.

If the trafficking ring might be as close as Langley, then she needed to be even more vigilant when it came to Tracy. Her niece wouldn't like having the strings tightened. She still complained about not being able to have a social-media presence under an assumed name with an avatar as her profile picture.

The ring she and Mason had brought down was

smarter than most gave them credit for. A predator might not know it was Tracy, but they would know the profile belonged to a young girl. Taya couldn't take that chance.

The doorbell rang. She grabbed the money from the table and opened it.

Sheriff Westbrook stood on the porch, his hat in hand. "Mind if I come in?"

~

"What's up?" Ryan stepped from the bedroom while buttoning his shirt.

Tracy joined him, one hand on Betty's head.

"Is there somewhere we can talk without…?" The sheriff tilted his head.

"Ugh." Tracy whirled and stomped to her room.

"Sounds serious. We can go in here." Ryan started to lead him to the living room when the door rang again. "Pizza." He took the money from Taya, leaving her to take the sheriff into the other room while he paid for the delivery. Hot pizza in hand, he set it on the coffee table. "Help yourself, Sheriff."

"No, thanks, but you might want to appease Tracy by taking her a slice or two."

"I will." Taya retrieved some paper plates from the kitchen, put two slices of pepperoni pizza on one of them, and headed down the hall, returning within a minute. "You didn't start without me, did you?"

"Wouldn't dream of it." Ryan bit into a slice. A string of hot cheese caught on his chin, and he hissed, then pulled it off. "Okay, Sheriff. You have our undivided attention."

The sheriff perched on the edge of the sofa. "Three girls, all matching the description of Tracy, have disappeared from Langley. The latest was last night from a dance studio. This leads us to believe the trafficking ring is in our county. I've called in the FBI." He glanced at Taya. "Can you get ahold of the group you worked with?"

She shook her head. "It disbanded with the death of our leader." She folded her hands in her lap. "I have been in contact with another group, but they work mostly online gathering information rather than field work." She took a deep breath. "However, they've asked me to do some investigating in Langley."

"Did you plan on telling me this?" Ryan frowned. Was she keeping secrets from him?

"I literally found out fifteen minutes ago, and I haven't decided what I'm going to do yet. My concern is Tracy."

"With your expertise, we could use you in the field." The sheriff rose to his feet. "Think about it. You could be an asset to the FBI when they arrive. Ryan can watch your niece."

Didn't he get a say in any of this? He couldn't keep both Tracy and Taya safe if they were split up. "I'm not military or law enforcement, Sheriff, and although I've read a lot of books, that doesn't qualify me to be a bodyguard to a teenage girl who will resent my attention."

"Are you regretting your decision to help these two?"

"Of course not. But, you're asking a lot of me. I don't have the training. A fake marriage in order to give them new identities is one thing, but to watch Tracy while Taya is out in the field is another." His worse fear was about to become a reality. He was going to fail at what he'd set out to do—to keep them both safe.

Taya cut him a sharp glance. "This ring has to be stopped."

"I know that." He shot to his feet and paced the room. "Let me at least think about this."

"Maybe we could find an undercover officer to stay here with you and help guard the girl." The sheriff clapped his hat on his head. "I'm sorry for springing this on you, but if that ring is in Langley, it could come here. My duty is to protect the citizens of this town. The cowboys from the Rocking W Ranch will take shifts patrolling the town. We will keep this ring out of Misty Hollow." With a nod, he left the house.

Ryan turned to Taya. "What are you going to do?"

~

"Boss, I seen that girl you're looking for." Hank rushed to where Bill sat in a folding chair, beer in hand. "Her hair is different, but it's the same face. I swear."

"I'm listening." He took a big swig.

"They took shelter in the bathroom near my camper during the storm."

"Today?" Bill frowned.

"Yep."

"And you're now just telling me this?" He tossed the bottle into the firepit. It shattered against a rock.

"I had work to do." He rocked back on his heels. "They took off when the worst of the storm stopped."

"They?"

"A man, a woman, and a black lab. They ran to the parking lot. I didn't get a look at what they were driving. They might have been hiking."

Bill shot to his feet and stood almost close enough to Hank for their noses to touch. "Did you identify the girl going in or coming out?"

The man swallowed hard enough for his Adam's apple to bob. "I thought it might be her when they went in but knew for sure when they came out. You told me to take my turn at the gate when the storm quit. So, I did, and now I'm here. Since I don't know where they went, I didn't think there was an urgency."

"You don't get paid to think. Get out of my sight." Bill's hands clenched into fists. It took all his willpower not to beat the man unconscious.

The girl had been right there! If Hank had said something, she'd be in Bill's hands at this moment—she and Taya. He didn't know who the man was; nor did he care. Now, he'd have to use valuable resources hiring more men to be out there looking.

They could be hiding in any of the small towns surrounding this mountain. Folks probably came from all around to enjoy the lake.

"Got three girls in the last twenty-four hours." Jason grinned as he approached. "They're all waiting for your approval."

"Tell me you didn't take them all from the same city."

"All three from Langley." Jason took a step back. "They were easy pickings, Boss."

Were any of his men able to follow orders? "I told you to spread it out. Now, you've basically wiped that city off the map for us."

"There are plenty of other towns, Boss. Lots of places out in the boondocks. It'll just take some driving around." The young man's smile remained despite the wary look in his eyes. "I won't let you down. Wanna see the new girls?"

"Of course, I do." It was the best part of the job. He followed Jason to one of the portable buildings.

Bill glanced in the direction of the farthest bathroom. If only he'd known. He had big plans for Taya and her niece. The young girl would fetch a high price, and her aunt would belong to him one way or another.

# Chapter Twelve

**Taya didn't answer** Ryan's question until the next morning. It wasn't that she intended to put him off, but she really hadn't made her final decision. More time on her laptop decided for her. "I'm going to Langley." She closed the computer. "Will you keep an eye on Tracy?"

Ryan stared at her without speaking. A muscle ticked in his jaw. He took a deep breath, then exhaled slowly. "So, you've decided."

"Yes."

"You aren't going without me, which means you aren't going without Tracy. I'll get my shoes." Before she could argue, he'd sprang to his feet and disappeared into his bedroom. "Tracy, get ready. We're heading to Langley."

Taya frowned. The other two were absolutely not going with her. It was too dangerous. She stood ready to do battle when Ryan returned. "No."

"Stop me." He shoved water bottles into his backpack, tossed in some granola bars, then pulled the fixings for sandwiches from the fridge. "I'm assuming we'll be there all day?"

"I will be there all day."

"Are we going to question the parents of the missing girls? Find a pattern?"

"I will be questioning them, yes." She planted her fists on her hips. Was the man deaf? No, merely the most stubborn person she'd ever met. "You. Are. Not. Going."

"If we don't go with you, we'll follow you. Short of shooting me, I'm taking Tracy to Langley."

"It's too dangerous." She stepped in front of him, so he'd be forced to look at her.

"Yes, it is."

"You're putting my niece in danger."

"She's in danger here. We might as well all stay together." He slapped jelly on a slice of bread. "I'm not a fan of PB & J, but it'll suffice in case we don't have time to grab a burger."

"Listen to me!" Taya rarely raised her voice, but sheer frustration rose.

"I am listening. Are you?" He set down the knife he used to spread peanut butter. "You need backup. I can stay in the Jeep with Tracy. I'll make sure her hair is stuck up under a ball cap. It needs to be redyed by the way. So does yours. I'll stay back unless you need me." He held up a hand. "I promise to stay back, but I am not letting you go alone." He ran his fingers through his hair. "I know I'm not really your husband and can't make you do anything—"

"You couldn't even if you were." She narrowed her eyes.

"But…the sheriff assigned me the task of bodyguard. I can't guard you if I'm not there."

"You have peanut butter in your hair." She reached up and smeared it into the tresses. "Sorry. I made it worse. Fine." She whipped around and marched to her room to get her weapon and ammo. With a huff, she leaned against the bed. No one in a very long time had cared enough about her to dig in their feet like Ryan just did. She smiled. Knowing he'd do anything in his power to keep her and Tracy safe warmed her heart. Maybe they'd succeed at this after all. Then what?

Could she stay in Misty Hollow with Tracy? See what the future might hold for her and Ryan? She shook her head. Why would she think that? He'd never made a single mention of them being anything more than what they were—two people after a common goal.

Once she had her gun secured in a shoulder holster, she headed back to the living room where Ryan and Tracy awaited. "Both of you, listen to me. You stay in the Jeep. No matter what. Understood?"

Ryan nodded, his features grim.

"Tracy?"

"Sure. Whatever. Come on, Betty." She yanked the front door open.

Taya shook her head and followed, not wanting to let her out of sight. She'd given up on warning Tracy not to go outside until the coast was clear. If Astro and Boris weren't acting as if something wasn't right, she let it be.

In the passenger seat of the Jeep, she punched the first address into her phone. "When you reach Langley, take the second exit."

"Yes, ma'am." He backed away from the house and headed down the mountain.

She cut him a sideways glance. From the curtness in his voice, it wasn't hard to determine that he wasn't happy with her. "The sheriff asked for my help."

"Hmpff."

"This is too important to say no."

"Uh-huh."

"Why are you so upset?"

He jerked the steering wheel to the right and parked on the side of the road before turning to her. "Because I care about you. Is that so difficult for you to see? I don't want anything to happen to you or Tracy."

He cared about her. She opened her mouth, then snapped it closed, not knowing what to say. Instead, she nodded like an idiot and stared at her phone.

"Wow," Tracy muttered from the backseat. "Talk about awkward."

Taya giggled.

Ryan laughed and pulled back onto the road.

*Thank you, Tracy, for your snarkiness.*

"Do you have experience questioning grieving parents?" Ryan asked.

"Not much. I usually stayed in the shadows and shot the bad guys." Which she preferred rather than sitting across from parents worried sick about their child. "I suppose you don't either?"

"No. I make that kind of stuff up as I go." He pulled onto the interstate. "Just be empathetic. Don't make light of their suffering, and don't make promises you can't keep."

She nodded, dreading the task more with every mile they drove. When Ryan took the second exit, she continued giving directions until they pulled in front of a red-brick house on an established, residential street. She shoved her door open. "Wish me luck."

"Good luck." He smiled. "We'll be here waiting for you."

Knowing he waited gave her strength. With heavy steps, she climbed the porch steps and pressed the doorbell.

A man who looked to be in his forties answered the door. "If you're selling something, you're wasting your time." He started to close the door.

"No, sir, Mr. West. I'm here on behalf of the Misty Hollow PD."

His brow furrowed. "Why? I've already spoken to the Langley police."

"They've asked for my help in finding your daughter. May I come in?"

"What can you do that they can't?"

"Find your daughter." Tracy stood at the bottom of the steps, a frustrated Ryan behind her.

He shrugged. "Sorry. She ran out before I could stop her."

Tracy moved closer. "She can find her the same way she found me."

The man glanced from Tracy to Taya and back again. "Okay. Come in."

"I told you to stay in the car." Heat climbed Taya's neck. She groaned and followed the man inside. So much for promises she might not be able to keep. "Stay, Betty." Even the dog wouldn't mind her. Betty lay on the porch, head on her paws.

Inside, framed photos of the man, a woman, and a pretty teenage girl lined the mantel over the fireplace. Down a short hallway, Taya spotted more photos.

"Please. Sit. I'll go get my wife. She…spends a lot of time in bed." He shuffled away.

The three of them squeezed onto a striped sofa.

"I could tell he wasn't going to let you in." Tracy

crossed her arms. "So, I came to help. To give them some hope."

"What if I fail?" Taya gripped her phone hard enough to make her knuckles ache.

"You won't. Taya, you never fail."

Wishing she had her niece's optimism, she faced the doorway at the sound of footsteps.

"You can find my baby?" A red-eyed woman entered the room and made a beeline for the sofa. "This girl with you was taken?"

Taya took a deep breath. "This is my niece. Yes, she was taken a little over six months ago. It took me a while, but I did find her and rescued her, along with a few others. I'm hoping to do the same for your daughter."

"How much? We'll pay whatever you're asking."

Taya held up her hands. "No, you don't understand. I'm helping the police. I'm not doing this for profit. Do you mind if I ask you a few questions?"

"We'll tell you anything if it helps get Lacey back." The woman took her husband's hand and pulled him onto the matching loveseat. "Do you want to take notes?" She grabbed a small notepad from the end table and handed it to Taya.

The woman's eagerness and hope shone from weary eyes.

Taya's throat seized. She cleared it and opened the notepad. "Lacey. Blond. Blue Eyes. Any distinguishing marks?"

"She has a birthmark on her inside right elbow," the father said. "Kind of looks like the state of Texas if you use your imagination."

Taya wrote that down. "Where was she…taken?"

"From outside the dance studio. When she didn't call or arrive home on time, I went looking for her. My wife's car, a Nissan, was still parked in the lot. No one saw Lacey talking to anyone. No one saw her get into a vehicle. It's like she vanished." He glanced at Tracy. "Was it like that for you?"

Tracy nodded. "I was outside a coffee shop, except it was me and my best friend. A really cute guy came up and started talking to us. We didn't think anything of it when he started moving down the sidewalk. We just went with him. When we reached the corner, a white van pulled up, and two men jumped out. Before we knew what was happening, we were inside, blindfolded and tied up. It happened very fast."

"Was your friend rescued?" Mrs. West clenched her hands together in her lap.

"No. She became sick and died." Tracy wiped her eyes with her sleeve. "But a lot more were rescued."

"It shouldn't take as long to find Lacey," Taya said. "We know the ring is close. I'm fairly certain it's the same ring we thought we shut down in Oklahoma."

"But now they're here." Mr. West reclaimed his wife's hand.

"We believe so, yes."

He glanced at Ryan. "What's your part in all this, Mr. Boyne? Yes, I recognize you from your books."

Ryan gave a grim smile. "I'm the bodyguard."

The visits with the other two families proceeded pretty much the same. Tracy gave them hope, and Taya had to go along with the promises.

By the end of the day, exhaustion weighed on her so heavily each step she took seemed as if her feet had been encased in cement. As they drove back to Misty

Mountain, she reclined her seat and closed her eyes.

When they arrived at Ryan's cabin, she woke and sat up. "I'd hoped to stop by the sheriff's office."

"If you really want to speak to him, I'll call and ask him to meet us here. You're too tired." Ryan held out his hand to help her from the Jeep. "What's so important it can't wait until morning?"

"I think I might have an idea where the next girl might be taken from."

# Chapter Thirteen

As he placed the call to the sheriff, Ryan's gaze never left Taya, his eyes full of questions, as she rummaged through the drawers for a map. "He's on his way. Tell me what's going on." He peered at the map.

"I wish you had a map of Misty Hollow and the surrounding areas."

"Let me ask the sheriff." He dialed again, made the request, and disconnected. "He has one. Are you going to make me wait?"

"Yes. In the meantime, give me a list of where all the girls in the state have disappeared from. I know there's three from Langley, but we'll count that as only one."

"The sheriff can tell you that better than I can."

"Another reason to wait for him then." She flashed him a smile, then returned to the map.

"It's no use, Ryan. My aunt is like a pit bull when she's focused on something." Tracy plopped into a recliner and slung one leg over the arm of the chair.

"Ha ha." Taya spared her a quick glance, then held out her hand. "A red marker, please."

"I don't know if I have one."

"Any marker will work, although I prefer red.

Where is the sheriff?"

"It's only been five minutes." Ryan rummaged through the kitchen drawers, then headed down the hall. When he returned, he dropped a blue marker on the table. "Sorry. No red."

She circled Misty Hollow, then drew a bigger circle around Misty Mountain. Once The Boss found out where they were hiding, this would become the center of his operations. Her gut told her he already suspected they were on the mountain somewhere. It was only a matter of time before he found them. They needed to prepare this place like a fortress.

"Instead of sleeping, your mind was going over all…this?" Ryan waved a hand over the map.

"Yes."

A knock sounded at the door, and he went to let the sheriff in.

"Brought the map."

"Great." Taya snatched it from his hand. "Now, I need a list of every missing girl in the last month."

"Let me call the office." He stepped out of the room and made the call. "Doris will text it to me, but it might take a few minutes. Can you tell me what you have while we wait?"

"I can, but I can't be certain I'm right without that list." She straightened. "I think Misty Hollow is the center of the targets. Which means—" She met his gaze.

"The ring is here."

She nodded. "How much do you want to bet it's the group at the campground? Where else could someone hide in plain sight?"

"Anywhere on this mountain?"

"Do you have another group of men who recently arrived?" She arched a brow.

"No." He muttered something under his breath and glanced at his phone screen. "I have the list."

Ryan handed him paper and a pencil. "Let's see whether Taya's hunch is right."

When Sheriff Westbrook had scribbled down the list, he slid it across the table to Taya. "I hope you're wrong. If not, I'm going to hang up my hat and hand over my badge."

"FBI here yet?" She started circling the places where the girls had gone missing.

"Tomorrow."

"Good. We'll have something to show them." She turned the map so they could see and tapped the center with the marker in each spot a girl had gone missing, then on Misty Hollow. She'd drawn a perfect triangle. "It won't be long until someone from this town is taken. Maybe in town, maybe outside city limits, but it will be close."

Ryan and the sheriff bent closer to the map. After a couple of minutes, the sheriff straightened, his features hard. "I have some calls to make. You three be careful." He strode from the house.

"My guess is he's gathering together enough people to pay a visit to the campground." Taya wished she were one of them. She'd give almost anything to face The Boss down the barrel of her rifle.

"Now what?" Ryan sat across from her, motioning his head toward the living room. "She's been hanging on every word you said."

"Tattletale." Tracy tossed a throw pillow at him.

"We need to fortify this place. They'll be coming if

the sheriff isn't successful in rounding them up. The dogs are a great warning system, but they can't keep several men from bombarding this place."

"Booby traps," Tracy called out.

"This isn't a movie." Taya shook her head.

"She might have something. Maybe we can't dig trenches, but we can put out traps that will give us a head start. We also need to come up with an escape plan." Ryan bolted to his feet. "Be right back."

~

Bill listened as one of his scouts informed him of Taya and the girl visiting the parents of the girls missing from Langley. It wouldn't take someone with Taya's brains long to figure out he was in town. "Prepare to leave. I'll let you know where in ten."

Because nothing was easy, he'd made a plan B before overtaking the campground. One of his men's relatives owned a farm several miles out of town. The farm was secluded enough and large enough they could hide there with no one the wiser. Several chicken houses would hide the campers. A barn would house the men. The house had several bedrooms in which they could stash the girls.

He grabbed a walkie-talkie from his table and let the others know before calling for Jason and Hank to help him vacate the campground. If anything went wrong, Bill wanted to make sure he was nowhere near the place.

Most likely, they should've gone there in the first place, but there were neighbors who might notice a convoy of campers driving past. They'd have to be taken care of before the largest part of the group arrived. Bill made another call to a few other men and gave them orders to clear out the two farms they'd have to pass, and another call with orders to gather the girls into a vehicle and out to the farm.

"Make sure the neighbors' bodies can't be easily found. If you can make it look like an accident, all the better." The more dead bodies, the harder it would be to hide. Thus, the main reason for the campground. They'd only had to dispose of the host.

What he'd really like to do is have the freedom to run his business. But, Taya had ruined that. She and her niece. The girls could ruin it all for him.

That's why Bill felt like a prisoner. Why he'd not left the campground since arriving. Why he'd be stuck at the farm same as he was here. Because accidents happened, and he wasn't about to be seen by anyone. What he needed was to get his hands on that girl!

"Ready, Boss." Hank poked his head through the open doorway. "One of the others will drive the camper. Ready?"

"Yes." He followed the man to the truck idling outside and took a last glimpse around the campground bustling with his men. Satisfied with how they were following orders, he climbed into the passenger seat of the truck.

On the way to the next destination, he thought of a way to bring Taya out of hiding.

~

"Okay." Ryan plopped a duffel bag on the table. "I only have a couple of handguns. You have a rifle. This won't be enough."

Taya's eyes widened. "We can't go to war in your front yard."

"I'm hoping we won't have to."

"Your writer's mind is running off on a tangent. If The Boss or his men show up here, we run. We do not get into a shootout."

"Again, I'm hoping we won't have to. I've researched warning systems for one of my books." Ryan sat down and pulled his laptop in front of him. "Let me read back over it and come up with a plan." He pulled up the needed file and read over it.

In his book, he'd used the standard empty aluminum cans, a trigger that sounded a shrieking alarm. He'd even used the cliché net tossed over the bad guys. All these tactics might run off an intruder or two. At the least, slow them down enough for the three in the cabin to make their escape.

Ryan glanced to where the three dogs lay in a circle around Tracy's chair. He didn't want them to go too far from the cabin anymore. They needed to stay close by where they couldn't be poisoned or harmed in any other way. He might not have experience with "The Boss," but the man wouldn't entertain a second thought about harming an animal. Not if he didn't value the lives of young girls.

"I can get more guns." Taya crossed her arms. "I still have a contact with the group I once belonged to. They'll have anything we need." She lowered her voice. "I still don't think it's a good idea considering we have—." Her head tilted toward her niece.

"What are the options then?" He sat back and gave her his full attention.

She shrugged. "We run again. If we're lucky, the man will give up."

"You don't really believe that." He leaned back, his eyes studying her. Did she? A man that ruthless would never give up. Not when someone could identify him. He huffed a sigh. "Let's prepare the best we can and hope the FBI and sheriff's department handle it."

"This man has eluded capture for years, Ryan. What makes you think this time will be any different?"

"Optimism. Faith." He'd grab at any straw. "From what I've heard, this town has been to hell and back before, but it always comes out ahead of evil. It will this time, too."

"I wish I believed that." Sorrow crossed her face. "More children have disappeared, never to be seen again, than have been rescued. Law enforcement and special forces all across this country have tried to put a stop to the trafficking. It's happening in America's backyard. I don't think it will stop. It's more lucrative than the drug trade."

"Then why fight it?" He tilted his head. "If there's no hope, why keep trying?"

"For that one child who can be saved." Hands flat on the table, she pushed to her feet. "I'll contact my source." With that, she left the room and stepped onto the back deck, pulling her phone from her pocket.

His gaze locked on the door she'd exited. He couldn't fight without the hope of winning the battle. He glanced at the few guns on the table. Maybe trouble wouldn't come to the cabin, but he knew it would. They needed to be ready for the worst, and sitting around wasn't going to prepare for anything.

"I think you should build a pit or hide those spikes that get triggered when someone trips a wire." Tracy stood in the doorway. "The traffickers are not nice people."

He bit back a smile at the seriousness on her face.

"I'd rather not clean up the mess. That would take time we might not have."

She nodded. "So, what are you going to do?"

"Set up warnings so we know they're coming. Let me show you something." He pushed to his feet and led her to a closet at the end of the hall. "This is where I want you to go if they come. Don't worry about me and your aunt. It's you they want."

He shoved aside some boxes, revealing a trap door. "I found this the day I moved in. Didn't think I'd ever need it."

"A cellar?"

"Most likely for tornadoes." He lifted the door. Stretching down were a set of stairs. He entered and pulled a chain that lit up the space. "I'll make sure there's a flashlight on the top step. If you're hiding, you shouldn't turn on the light. It'll show."

"Okay." Her reply was hushed. "Can I bring Betty?"

He glanced over his shoulder. "Absolutely." The dog might very well be the girl's last line of defense if something happened to him and Taya. At the very least, her bark will be a warning.

"Why haven't you shown us this before?"

"I haven't needed to. No storms." The storm coming was worse than anything Mother Nature could throw at them. "It was probably used as a root cellar for canning." He pointed to a rack of shelves. "We'll make sure you have food and water until help comes for you."

"How long will I be down here?" Her voice rose. "I'd rather fight than hide down here. I don't like…this."

He turned to face her. "You might not have a choice, Tracy. This could be the only thing to save you when they come."

"They'll see the moved boxes."

"Not if I secure the boxes to the door. When you pull it closed, it'll look as if nothing was disturbed."

"You've thought of everything."

He certainly hoped so. If not, they could all perish.

# Chapter Fourteen

**Ryan really did** think of everything. Taya blinked back tears. He truly cared about her niece and would do whatever was in his power to keep her safe.

She stepped onto the stairs leading to the cellar. "My contact will meet us in the parking lot of Lucy's Diner in two hours. I'd like to go into town and stock up on supplies in case we're stuck here."

"Okay." Ryan stood at the bottom of the stairs. "We can put some blankets and stuff down here, too. Just in case."

A wonderful idea she prayed they wouldn't need. She moved back and waited for the other two to join her. "The closet seems a weird place for a storm shelter."

"It looks like this part of the house was built on after the fact. See?" He ran his hand over a seam in the wall. "This closet and the back bedroom are newer. So, since the cellar makes no sense being in the closet, it's perfect."

A quiet Tracy pushed past them, Betty on her heels.

"She doesn't like the idea," Ryan said.

"I don't imagine she does." Neither did Taya. The

thought of hiding her niece underground made her stomach roll. What if she couldn't make it back to rescue her?

Ryan ordered his two dogs to stay in the yard, then held out his hand for the keys. "Feed my ego and let me drive."

Taya laughed. "You don't have an ego." She dropped the keys in his palm.

Once inside the Jeep, he asked, "How can your contacts be here so fast? It's at least four hours from Oklahoma City."

"I never said they were in OKC." She tilted her head. "But they were until they received a tip that there's a trafficking ring close by my location." It bothered her that the group had kept tabs on her. She'd asked that they let her go for Tracy's safety. So much for favors.

He frowned. "Did everyone know the ring's location except for us and local law enforcement?"

"We know now." All they had to do was find them before they found Tracy.

"What kind of supplies? Food? Water?"

"Is there someplace to get infrared goggles? A Kevlar vest? Those types of things?"

His eyes widened. "You going out into the field?"

"If they come to the cabin, I plan on coming up behind them." She hitched her chin. "It's what I do, and I'm very good at my job."

"I don't live here, so I have no idea where someone would buy that kind of stuff."

"I'll look online for a military surplus store." Minutes later she found one in Langley. "If we hurry, we'll have time to make my appointment."

Ryan nodded and pulled onto the interstate. "Best to get the groceries after the meeting in case it goes long."

"It won't." She should've asked her contact to bring the goggles and vest along with guns and ammo, but it had slipped her mind. Preparing for war had thrown her off kilter. Or, at least, some semblance of war. When had things gone so wrong? Answer—When her sister died and left her to raise a preteen. Taya hadn't been qualified. Her job took her away too often, leaving Tracy unsupervised. Then, Taya had quit after the rescue, only to find herself right back where she started—going out to fight and leaving her niece behind.

"What's wrong?" Ryan cut her a sideways glance.

"That's a dumb question."

"I mean right now. This instant."

"Second-guessing my decision to take Tracy in."

"You did great, Taya." Tracy put a hand on her shoulder. "You saved my life."

Tears burned. "I might not be able to a second time."

"Yes, you will." After a clap on her shoulder, Tracy sat back. "You always tell me to believe in myself. Take your own advice."

A laugh escaped Ryan. "I guess she told you."

"I guess she did." Taya smiled, feeling better. She could do this. No, *they* could do this. She wouldn't accomplish anything by going solo.

The surplus store in Langley had everything she needed. She bought an extra vest for Ryan and a lantern for Tracy to take into the cellar with her if she had to go down there.

Ryan eyed the purchases. "You think I'll need that? A shooter can go for the head and totally bypass the vest."

"A vest is still handy." She tossed the bag into the back of the Jeep. "Humor me."

"I'm not special ops, Taya." He dropped another bag next to hers.

"Pretend it's research." She closed the back and slid into the front passenger seat, then glanced at her watch. They'd make it with ten minutes to spare barring heavy traffic on the interstate.

When Ryan pulled into the lot of the diner, Taya scoured the area. "There." She grinned, recognizing both Lance and Nora from her former group. "You two stay in the vehicle. It's safer for them if people don't see them."

As she exited the Jeep, her friends moved to the side of the diner out of sight of the street. Taya rushed to catch up with them. "Thank you." She made a move to hug Nora, only to have her take a step back. The icy look on the woman's face froze Taya. "What?"

Lance dropped a duffel bag at her feet. "Tell me you aren't going to use these against law enforcement."

She frowned. "What are you talking about?"

He searched her face for a minute. "You really don't know?"

"Know what?" She glanced from one to the other. "I don't have time for games, Lance."

"Mason is alive."

"What?" She took a step back. "No. I saw him fall."

"A ruse. The two who pulled him from sight were in on it. Mason is the leader of the ring. How could you not know that?" He narrowed his eyes. "The two of you were close. Very close if rumors are true."

"The rumors are wrong. We were never more than friends." Although Mason had tried many times to convince her to be more. Mason was alive? The leader of the ring? She shook her head. "But…we saved those girls. He helped us."

"All a ploy to keep us from catching him sooner." Nora crossed her arms.

"How do you know this?"

"No record of his death. No record of his injuries. Nothing. It's as if Mason ceased to exist. Only someone who didn't want to be found would erase themself."

Taya picked up the bag, happy for the weight. Anger roiled through her like billowing waves. "I will bring him down."

"Wish we could help," Lance said, "but we're on a different assignment. Be careful, Taya. He's going to be a cornered panther."

And she would be an African lion protecting her pride.

~

A very quiet, very serious Taya returned to the Jeep. If not for the determined glint in her eyes, Ryan might have thought she'd given up. "Find out what you needed?"

"More than I needed, actually." She turned slightly in her seat to face him. "I just found out that my friend and former leader of the ops group is not dead. In fact, he's very much alive and the leader of this trafficking ring. Which means, Tracy isn't the only one who can identify him. I can, too. Tracy doesn't have to be anywhere near this now."

"You're sending me away?" Tracy leaned over the seat. "To where? I'm not going."

"Nobody is going anywhere, right?" He gripped the steering wheel. "We're in this together."

"I don't know where I'd send her anyway. Let's head to the sheriff's office. If the FBI has arrived, then I can give them my assessment and see whether they have a safe house for Tracy and someone to watch her."

"I'm not going!" She reached for her door.

Ryan hit the lock button.

"I'll run away. I promise." Tears ran down her cheeks. "You can't leave me again, Taya."

"No one is leaving anyone." Ryan turned the Jeep around, coming to a halt as two cowboys on horseback crossed the lot entrance.

"Who are they?" Tracy's tears dried in a heartbeat.

"They're helping the sheriff monitor the town."

"I've never seen anyone more handsome." She pressed her face to the side window. "I'm going to marry a cowboy someday."

Taya's eyes widened. She covered her mouth to hide her grin. "That was a fast switchover."

Ryan shrugged. "Guess all it takes to make her happy is a man on a horse."

"Isn't that the way with most women?" Taya's grin widened.

Relieved some of the tension had been erased, he drove to the sheriff's office. The parking lot was a beehive of activity as men in black raced in the front door.

"Something happened." Ryan shoved his door open. His heart shot to his throat.

"A girl was taken. Either that or they've located

the ring. Those are the only two things I can think of that would generate this response." Taya exited the Jeep, grabbing a large bag as she did, and then opened the back door for Tracy. "Looks like groceries will have to wait a bit longer."

They followed the FBI into the building.

Sheriff Westbrook turned from the front desk. "Ryan, Taya, come with me."

Tracy plopped onto a chair, Betty lying at her feet, while Ryan and Taya followed the sheriff.

"Have a seat." The sheriff motioned to a couple of empty chairs at the conference table. "This is Special Agents Snow and Larson. Needless to say, they arrived in the middle of chaos."

"Who was taken?" Taya leaned forward. "Someone from Misty Hollow?"

He nodded. "You were right. The ring hit here this morning. It's too early to know for sure, but a teenage girl didn't make it to school today. There's no record of her having gotten on the bus. Her parents say she's never skipped school before, so we need to assume the worse. At our last calculations, there are five girls missing."

"You have something for us?" Agent Larson arched a brow at Taya.

"More than I thought." Taya pulled the map from the large purse she carried with her. "Center of operations. But, this isn't all." She reached over and gripped Ryan's hand under the table.

"Mason Rogers isn't dead."

"And he is?" Larson pursed his lips.

"My former special ops partner. I met with a couple of my old group this morning and found out he faked his death. They believe he is the leader of this ring. They also believe he's in Misty Hollow."

"Since the campground is empty," Sheriff Westbrook said. "It's safe to assume the ring is here and right under our noses."

~

"The woman and kid are at the sheriff's office."

Mason, aka The Boss, frowned at his phone. "You're sure it's them?"

"Yep. They're with a man and a black dog."

"Follow them when they leave. I want to know where they're staying."

"So, leave the girl I'm watching?"

"Yes." Mason gripped the phone so hard he thought he might crack the screen.

"Uh…before that they were meeting with a rough-looking man and woman at the diner. They gave the woman you're looking for a duffel bag. It looked heavy. I couldn't hear what they said, but whatever it was made the gal really upset."

Mason cursed, then hung up. Taya must've met with some of the old group—ones who knew about his deception. With his cover blown, it wouldn't take long for the feds to show up at the farm. They'd search every inch of the area until they found him. He needed to go into hiding until he could nab Taya and the girl. Someone else would have to take over for a while. Let that person take the fall when the feds arrived. He had enough money stashed to live off of comfortably for a long time. What he'd get for the girl would set him up even longer.

Yup, it was definitely time to go. He headed for his room and packed a bag before going in search of his next-in-command. "I need to go. My cover is blown. You're in charge for now. I'll be in touch." With that, he strode to the large red barn, tossed his bag in the front seat of an older model Ford truck, and spun gravel on his way out.

# Chapter Fifteen

Taya sipped a cup of coffee the next morning, staring at the woods behind Ryan's cabin. Today, he planned on setting his "booby" traps as Tracy called them. Alarms were a more apt description. Either way, it wouldn't deter Mason. He always got what he wanted.

Sleep had been a long time coming the night before as she lay there still in shock that he had faked his death. They'd worked together for years. How long had he been on the wrong side of the law? Of morality? She'd almost said yes to a relationship with the man. Was he that good of a con man, or was she simply stupid? Taya slammed her cup hard enough on the railing of the deck to break off the handle. The cup tipped, spilling hot coffee down the front of her jeans. She hissed and jumped back.

"Here." Ryan quickly came to her aid and handed her a dish towel. "Are you okay?"

"Hopefully, I will be someday." She wiped the coffee off herself the best she could and handed him back the towel, her gaze clashing with his concerned one. She wanted to ask him what secrets hid behind those blue eyes. With her track record, she'd never figure it out herself.

His gaze dropped to her mouth before he cleared his throat and stepped back. "Would you like another cup of coffee?"

"No, thank you." Her voice sounded husky to her ears.

"What?" His brow furrowed.

"Are you really as good as you seem?"

His lips curled into a slow, sexy smile. "I like to think so."

"Why did you so readily agree to help us?" He could be keeping watch on them until Mason was ready to take Tracy. Groomers. She'd heard of such people before.

He put his hands on her shoulders. "Because I'm a sucker for a beautiful woman in trouble." His smile started to fade, and his hands slipped free. "Do you not trust me, Taya?" Pain flickered in his eyes.

"I want to," she whispered. She wanted to have someone she could trust more than anything in the world, second to keeping Tracy safe.

He cupped her face and lowered his head. His words caressed her lips a mere breadth before his kiss. "You can trust me."

Closing her eyes, she leaned into his kiss, giving into the feeling of nothing more than that moment. A moment she might never have again. A moment when nothing else existed but the two of them. She wrapped her arms around his neck and moved closer.

His hands dropped to her waist. The kiss deepened. When both of them were breathless, Taya stepped back. What now? Should she thank him or simply go about her day as if the kiss hadn't happened?

The sparkle in his eyes gave her the answer. "Wow."

"Yeah." She smiled. "Doesn't mean I completely trust you, Ryan. It only means that you're a great kisser."

His laugh rang out. Astro and Boris raised their heads. Boris whined, then laid his head back on his paws.

Ryan sobered and took Taya's hand in his. "I'd die for you. Surely you know that."

She gave a slow nod, wanting to believe him, knowing she'd do the same for him. When had she started to have these feelings for him? They seemed to have always been there, simmering low inside her. "What horrible timing."

"Me dying for you?" He tilted his head.

"No, silly. This." She motioned her hand between them.

"There will be a time life will return to normal."

She really hoped so. In the meantime, she had a job to do. "I'll keep watch while you set the alarms. Tracy should be okay with Betty if she stays in the house." Taya caressed his cheek, then went to fetch her rifle.

"It's about time." Tracy grinned and turned away from the window.

"You shouldn't be spying." Taya's face heated.

"What took y'all so long? When I meet the cowboy I'm going to marry, I plan on kissing him first thing."

"That would be…forward. As for me and Ryan, there's too much going on to pursue a relationship."

"The two of you are already married, sort of. You live together, wake up in the same house, eat all your meals together." She shrugged. "You might as well make it official."

"Again, it's not the time." Taya smiled as she headed to the room she shared with her niece.

A few minutes later, dry clothes on, a rifle over her shoulder, and extra ammo in her pocket, she headed back to the kitchen. "Lock the doors and stay inside. If you hear gunfire, head for the cellar. Keep Betty with you at all times."

"You think they'll come today?"

"No, sweetheart, I don't, but we have to be prepared." She had no idea when Mason would show his face.

~

Mason sat in his truck outside a farmhouse in the middle of a large field. So far, he hadn't seen anyone come and go other than an old man. Needing a place to hole up for a while, the secluded house seemed perfect. He grabbed his revolver from the passenger seat and exited the truck.

He hadn't gone anywhere near the house when an SUV pulled into the drive. Those inside turned to stare as they passed him. A woman and three young children. Mason cursed and climbed back into his truck. One old man was nothing, but an entire family would be noticed if they suddenly disappeared.

He drove further down the dirt country road. He slowed at every trail or what might have been a road he passed, looking for a place to pull in and stay. Not for long. He planned on making his move as soon as he received the call informing him where Taya and the girl were hiding. Which should be any time now.

Actually, the fool should've called yesterday.

Mason frowned. Something had happened. Had he been caught with the girl?

He made a quick phone call. "Where are you?"

"At the farm. I had a flat. Then, the girl escaped, and I had to chase her down. Got her back, and now I'm dropping her off."

"Did you follow the woman and kid?"

"Yes. They're in a cabin on top of the mountain." The man gave the directions. "Also, the FBI is in town, and there's a bunch of cowboys riding up and down the streets. This ain't good, Boss. It might be time to head out."

"I'll tell you when it's time." Mason disconnected and rubbed his chin. He'd hoped to have more time before the feds arrived. If they were watching where Taya hid, it would make it hard for him to get to her. Unless he waited until she went into town. A great risk to him.

~

With a burlap bag he'd found in the garage slung over his shoulder, Ryan headed down the deck steps.

Taya chuckled. "You look like the strangest Santa I've ever seen."

"A sack full of fishing twine and empty cans doesn't make very nice gifts." He gave her a quick kiss as he passed—something he intended to do at every opportunity. It still hurt that Taya had said she might not trust him. What could he do to prove she could? He stifled a sigh. Only time would tell.

The dogs went ahead of him, stopping at the edge of the woods when Ryan called out to them, "Watch." The dogs sat at alert.

Taya stood, rifle ready a few feet away. "Let me

know if I can help."

"Just keep watch." It would take him a while to string the fishing line with the cans at ankle height. Anyone looking close enough would see the trip wire, but then they might not see the second wire that actually triggered an alarm in the cabin with a piercing shriek and flashing lights.

As he worked, he told Taya about the inside alarm.

"When did you get those?"

He grinned. "When we were at the surplus store. I couldn't resist something so James Bondish."

"I'm sure it'll scare the dickens out of us if it goes off."

No doubt, but they'd at least have warning someone was coming. Even a short warning could mean the difference between capture and freedom.

He snuck a peek at Taya. In her camouflage pants and army-green tee-shirt, black sunglasses, and rifle over one arm, she looked every bit the warrior. The set of her jaw, the rigidness of her back—all said she was ready to take on anything that might come their way. While Ryan wanted to protect Taya, it well could be she who kept him safe. He trusted no one more to make sure they all made it out of this alive.

From the woods, the sheriff appeared along with Snowe and Larson marching across the cleared section of land in his direction. He wiped his hands on his jeans and motioned his head to Taya.

"What now?" She glanced at him.

"I don't know, but it's never good when Sheriff Westbrook shows up. At least not lately."

They waited side by side for the three to reach them. Taya slid the hand not holding the rifle into

Ryan's.

"Sheriff." Ryan squared his shoulders. "Agents. What can we do for you?"

"There's no sign of the group from the campground," the sheriff said. "A cadaver dog did find the camp host's body. We'll be putting a chopper in the air. When we couldn't reach either of you by phone, we came out here." He narrowed his eyes. "May I ask what's going on?"

Ryan grinned. "Sorry. We left our phones in the cabin. This, Sheriff, is a simple, pre-warning alarm system."

"Where's Tracy?" He glanced back at the house.

"Inside." He sobered. "In the hall closet under boxes secured to the floor is a trap door leading to a cellar. If Mason Rogers or his men come here, or if Taya or I perish, that's where you'll find Tracy."

"Good to know. But, I don't anticipate anything happening to either one of you as long as you stay here. If you need groceries, call for delivery. You aren't safe in town. Too many places for Rogers and his men to hide and take you out." He glanced around the area. "I don't think you should be this far from the house. A sniper could take you out before you took your next breath."

"I agree," Agent Snowe said. "You're at risk out here. Not even the dogs could save you. I suggest you finish while we're here, then head back to the safety of the house."

"So, we're prisoners?" Taya sighed.

"Yes, ma'am, if that's what it takes to keep you safe."

# Chapter Sixteen

**The mountain hadn't** become the refuge Taya had sought. Instead, it became a trap. No way out except down the one road leading to Ryan's place or through the woods. Both of which would be watched by Mason or his men.

She sighed and continued her surveillance out the back window. Sitting on the deck wasn't considered safe anymore. Despite Ryan's "traps," anyone could approach the cabin and not be seen until they were practically knocking on the door. All it would take was to knock the dogs out for a while.

Ryan moved behind her and wrapped his arms around her waist. "Sleep okay?"

"Not really." She leaned back against him. "Too many what ifs running through my head." She turned and gazed into his face. "I want to draw Mason out. I want to end this. But…the danger's too great. So, we wait."

"It won't be long now."

"How do you know?"

"With all the heat on this mountain, the man will grow desperate. He'll make his move, and we'll nab him." He gave her a quick kiss before stepping back and pouring a cup of coffee.

"We're out of cereal." Tracy, arms crossed, hair mussed from sleep, stood in the kitchen doorway.

"Make a list. I'll call in a delivery." Ryan patted her head, receiving a scowl in return.

Taya bit back a laugh at her niece's indignation at being treated like a child. "We can have the cereal here today. In the meantime, can I fix you some eggs?"

"Whatever." She grabbed a pad of paper from a drawer and sat at the table. "I finished my schoolwork early."

"Great job." Taya tossed a smile Ryan's way, grateful he'd insisted Tracy take online classes so she didn't fall too far behind. "Next week, you can start the next course."

The girl groaned and kept writing.

A couple of minutes later, Taya made a call and placed the order for delivery. Still smiling, she turned back to the window. Something moved along the tree line.

Astro and Boris shot from under the deck and dashed to the trees.

The inside siren blared.

"Tracy, into the cellar." Ryan tossed Taya her rifle from the counter before grabbing his handgun.

"It's probably a possum."

"Tracy, now!" Taya glared over her shoulder. "It's not a possum. It's Mason." The man stepped from the trees and aimed a gun at the dogs. "Ryan, call them back. He won't hesitate to kill them."

Ryan opened the back door a couple of inches, then put his fingers to his mouth and let loose a piercing whistle. The dogs immediately stopped and returned to the house.

"That's him." Tracy's voice shook. "That's The Boss." She whirled and dashed down the hall.

"What's he doing?" Ryan let the dogs into the house, then closed the door.

"I don't know."

The man simply stood and stared at the house.

Did he want her to step outside? Was he simply trying to intimidate them?

"Don't go out there. He could have a sniper waiting."

How did he do that? Read her mind? "Then call the sheriff's office." Was this it? Was today the day it ended? She tightened her grip on the rifle. So be it. Let Mason come.

"The agents will be here as soon as they can."

"It won't be soon enough."

Mason sauntered toward the cabin, a humorless grin on his face.

Taya opened the window a crack and aimed her rifle. "Stop right there. You know what kind of a shot I am."

He held up his hands. "Let's talk."

"I've nothing to say to you." How could she not have seen the evil radiating off him?

"There's a lot to talk about, Taya." He laughed. "But it can wait." He gave a mock bow and backed up a few steps before heading back to the trees.

She reached for the door.

"No." Ryan shot out a hand to stop her.

"He's going to get away."

"Let the agents handle him. Please." His look implored her to do as he asked. "Don't go out there alone."

She nodded. "Can I at least shoot him?" She quirked her mouth.

"In the back?" He arched a brow, eyes twinkling.

"There you go, being all nice again." She lowered her weapon.

"I'll let Tracy know she can come out." He left her staring after the retreating Mason.

"You're okay." A few minutes later, Tracy threw herself into Taya's arms. "I thought I'd come out, and you'd be dead."

"I don't kill that easily." She wrapped her niece in a hug. "Thank you for doing as we asked."

"Seeing that man made me go. It brought back all the fear of being held captive." She buried her face in Taya's shoulders, her body trembling.

Taya propped her weapon against the wall. "Come on. Let's sit on the sofa and wait for the FBI agents."

~

Mason hadn't seen the girl, but he knew she was there. Taya wouldn't let her be far. From the shadows, he watched the cabin.

He'd almost expected a bullet in the back as he'd marched away, but he should've known Taya wouldn't have the guts to shoot a friend—former friend or not.

The house didn't seem to have any alarms once he moved past the trip wires. At least none that he could see. A poisoned slab of meat could easily take care of the dogs. Getting inside shouldn't be too difficult—not for a man of his cunning, anyway.

Staying well out of reach of Taya's gun, he moved through the trees looking for points of weakness. Soon, he'd bring a group of men and storm the cabin. The man living there was expendable. He only wanted the woman and the girl, and he would have them one way or the other.

No one got away from him. No one.

~

Sheriff Westbrook and the two FBI agents arrived within twenty minutes. "We'd like you three to stay inside while we check the perimeter."

Taya shook her head and stood. "I'm going with you."

"Taya." Ryan took a step toward her.

"This is what I do. Watch Tracy for me. Please." Without waiting for confirmation, she headed to her room and donned her Kevlar vest. It wouldn't stop a shot to the head, but it was better than no protection at all. She didn't trust Mason not to take a shot at her.

A terrified Tracy still sat on the couch. The beseeching look on her face almost made Taya change her mind. No, she couldn't. Finding Mason and stopping him was the only way to keep her niece and many other girls safe.

She gave Tracy a hug and promised to return. Before leaving she cupped Ryan's face. "Trust me."

"I do."

"I'll be back in a few." She nodded to the agents and squared her shoulders. "I'm ready. My rifle is by the back door."

"Then, we'll go out that way," Larson said. The others followed him outside.

As they trooped across the lawn, Taya glanced back. Ryan stood framed by the window and raised his hand in a wave before turning away. They'd be fine. If anyone could protect Tracy instead of Taya, it was

Ryan. The man didn't have battle experience, but he had a good head on his shoulders.

"Where did you see the man?" Snowe faced her.

"There. By the big oak. After he tripped the wire, he strode toward the house as if he planned on staying for supper." Taya glanced at the ground around the trip wire. "It's almost as if he knew the wire was here and didn't care." Which almost made her wish Ryan had dug a pit with spikes as Tracy suggested.

"A simple act of intimidation." Snowe stepped over the wire. "It looks like he went this way. Did it appear as if he were alone?"

"Yes. At least, I didn't see anyone else."

The agent nodded. "He's scouting, and he'll be back with reinforcements."

"I've called in for some officers from Langley to help on this case." The sheriff removed his hat, ran his hand through his hair, then replaced the hat. "We don't have near enough men to tackle the group if they become aggressive as one cohesive unit."

Taya stiffened. "Has the town ever experienced anything of this magnitude before?"

"We've had a gang war. That's about as close as we've come." He exhaled heavily. "I'm starting to think it's time for me to retire. Come on. Let's see what other clues this guy left us."

After circling the cabin and doing their best not to trample any potential evidence, it became clear that Mason was, indeed, scouting. Taya turned and stared at the cabin as he might have done. What had he seen?

The log cabin wouldn't fall easily, but its windows could be shattered, its doors busted open. They'd be guarding the front and back doors, which meant the cabin would be a virtual prison, leaving those inside at the mercy of the traffickers.

"We need to go somewhere else." She glanced at the sheriff. "We're sitting ducks on this mountain."

"We'll set up a safe house in town," Larson said. "I agree. This is not a safe place for you. You could hole up for quite a while, but if the cabin is torched, you can't get out without being caught."

"Let's tell Boyne." The sheriff led the way back to the house.

The group gathered on the deck after it became apparent Mason was no longer around. Sheriff Westbrook explained the need for them to leave the top of the mountain.

Ryan shook his head. "Someone needs to stay. Mason needs to believe that Taya and Tracy are still here. If he doesn't, he'll take the trouble into town, and innocent people will suffer."

"What are you proposing?"

"That I stay here."

"No." Taya would not allow that to happen. "Mason won't hesitate to kill you."

"I won't give him that opportunity. You take Tracy into town, and I'll stay here to keep his attention on this cabin."

"You need me, Ryan."

He put his hands on her shoulders and stared deeply into her eyes. "Yes, I do. Which is why this has to happen. I need you alive, not in the hands of that man. Think about Tracy."

The emotion pouring from his eyes strengthened her. He was right. Tracy was the top priority right now. She had to get her away from there. "Okay, but I don't have to like it."

"Good. We'll have someone pick you up in the morning. That gives us time to prepare the house. Be on guard tonight. Agent Snowe and Larson will stay with Boyne."

Hearing that relieved some of the fear clenching Taya's heart. "We'll be ready." She brushed past them and headed for the front door where Tracy stood talking to someone.

Taya rushed in front of her. "What are you doing?"

"Getting the delivery."

A handsome young man motioned to the bags at his feet. "You did place an order, right?"

Taya glanced past him, noting a small red sedan. How had he driven close without anyone hearing? "Yes. Thank you. You may go now." The look on her face sent him scurrying to his car. Taya whirled to face her niece. "How long has he been here?"

She lifted a shoulder. "I don't know. Twenty minutes, maybe. We were only talking. I knew you were a shout away." She grabbed one of the bags. "We did place an order, you know."

"Have you forgotten it was a handsome boy that abducted you?" Taya set her rifle inside the door and grabbed a couple of bags.

"Yes, but he wasn't a delivery boy." Tracy wrinkled her nose and carried the bag into the house.

Taya glanced over to see the tail end of the car disappear over the hill. How could she convince Tracy she couldn't trust anyone until Mason and his trafficking ring were locked away?

# Chapter Seventeen

At the wail of the alarm, Taya bolted from bed and reached for her weapon.

"Taya?" Tracy's wide eyes glowed in the moonlight coming through the slats of the blinds over the bedroom window.

"Let me check it out. You be ready to hide." Barefoot, she met Ryan in the hall. Together, they headed to the back door.

A window shattered.

Tracy screamed.

Footsteps pounded down the hall.

Taya whirled and sprinted back to the bedroom as Tracy pulled the hall closet door closed behind her. Good girl.

A rock lay in the middle of shards of glass on the bedroom floor.

Taya glanced at her bare feet, then shuffled sideways to her shoes. After shoving her feet into them, she crunched her way to the window and peered out. Nothing. No one.

Astro and Boris set up a frenzied barking from the living room.

"They're playing with us." Ryan peeked through

the blinds on the front window. "Someone ran across the front porch to rile the dogs up, then ducked out of sight."

"Can you tell how many?" She took up a position on the opposite side of the door.

"No."

"I can't leave you here alone, Ryan." Her throat clogged.

"I won't be alone. The feds will be with me. We'll hole up inside, bored out of our minds, while you and Tracy are safe in a house in town surrounded by handsome cowboys." He winked. The gesture did nothing to erase the worry lines on his forehead.

"The cowboys will be nice." She forced a smile. "Especially for Tracy."

One of the kitchen windows shattered.

"I'll keep lookout of the back. If you can get a shot off, take it." She marched to the back of the house.

"Not sure I can shoot someone."

Her steps faltered, and she turned. "Excuse me?"

He shrugged. "I've never shot a person before. Only shot one thing in my life, and it was a rattlesnake. Took me three shots to hit it, and it was only three feet away."

"And you want me to leave you?"

"You're one gun. The agents are two." He shrugged again. "I'm just giving you a heads-up."

"Well, I don't have the same qualms about shooting someone." She stood to where she could see out the kitchen window but out of the line of sight of anyone outside. The clock said five-thirty a.m. The agents couldn't arrive soon enough.

Torn between wanting to stay and keep Ryan safe

and moving Tracy out of danger, her mind whirled trying to find a way to do both. She came up empty. It was one or the other. Despite her growing feelings for Ryan, her niece still remained top priority. Keep Tracy safe, then find the other girls held captive. She'd deal with her heart later.

Taya narrowed her eyes as a man darted in and out of the trees. Not Mason. Was he out there, or had he sent his goons while he stayed safely out of harm's way? It didn't matter. She'd get to him soon enough, and only one of them would walk away. She intended that person to be her, God willing.

Did God answer prayers when it meant someone would die? Even someone like Mason? Another question for which she didn't have an answer.

Right before the sun kissed the top of the trees, the rock throwing stopped. No more men dashing through the trees. The hackles on the dogs' necks lay back in place.

Taya knocked on the cellar door. "All clear."

Tracy's tear-streaked face appeared. "I'm done with this."

"So am I, sweetie." She held out a hand to help her niece up the steps. "So am I. It'll all be over soon."

The crunch of gravel outside signaled the arrival of a car. A glance outside showed the two agents pulling up in a black SUV. Subtle.

Ryan stepped onto the porch and pointed to the unattached garage. Shaking his head, he returned to the house. "That vehicle would be a dead giveaway."

"And those two yahoos are going to be the ones protecting you?" She glanced down the road. "Sheriff is coming. Guess he's our ride. Finish packing, Tracy."

"I did last night." She sat on the sofa, her arms around Betty's neck.

"Then, I'll grab our bags." She cast Ryan a look, wanting to tell him—beg him—to come with them. Instead, she sighed and headed for the bedroom leaving all she wanted to say unsaid.

A backpack in one hand and another bag slung over her shoulder, she gripped a used suitcase they'd picked up in town, then she retrieved her rifle from the front room. "We're ready."

"In a minute." Ryan took all the bags and set them near the door. "I'd like to speak with you for a minute."

She nodded, her gaze locked on his.

He led her to the kitchen. "You weren't going to leave without saying goodbye, were you?"

Shaking her head, she swallowed against the boulder in her throat. "Of course not."

He leaned his forehead against hers. "I don't know when we'll see each other again. It might not be until this is over."

How would she bear it?

"Seeing you first thing in the morning, last thing before going to bed—these have been the best days of my life." His voice broke. "Promise me you'll stay safe. Don't be a hero."

She choked off a laugh. "But, I am a hero."

He cupped her face and claimed her gaze again. "Promise me."

"Okay. I promise not to do anything that doesn't absolutely need doing."

He chuckled. "I'll take it." He lowered his head and landed a kiss on her, so full of longing and fear that her knees weakened.

She wrapped her arms around his neck and reciprocated with all the promise she could put in a kiss.

"I don't mean to break up the lovefest," the sheriff said from the doorway. "But, the sun is rising. We don't want any more folks to see me dropping the two of you off than necessary."

"Okay." Taya stepped back. She caressed Ryan's cheek with the palm of her hand, then followed the sheriff, retrieving their meager belongings on the way.

As they pulled away from the house, she glanced back in time to see the front door close on what she hoped wasn't the final one. It had been a long time since she'd found a man she wanted to share a future with.

"He'll be okay." Tracy took her hand. "Ryan is the smartest person I know."

"I'm counting on that." She gave her niece's hand a gentle squeeze.

"What about us? We're going to be in town, surrounded by people, and we'll still have nothing to do."

"Maybe I can have someone pick you up some new books from the library."

Tracy sighed. "I'm getting tired of reading."

"What? I didn't think that was possible." She chuckled and gave her a one-armed hug.

"The safe house isn't completely ready." Sheriff Westbrook glanced in his rearview mirror. "It should be by tomorrow. The owner would rather take her child and let you two stay there alone. It has a safe room where you can lock yourself in if trouble comes."

Taya met his gaze. "Where then?"

He smiled. "You'll be staying with June Mayfield tonight. I guarantee neither of you will be bored."

"Aren't you putting the woman in danger?"

"Nope. Not a soul on this planet would dare harm a hair of that woman's head. She's the town's grandmother. If they did, the wrath of God would descend. We've also put a tracker on your phone, so please try to keep it with you at all times."

She nodded. He might have something. Who would expect two fugitives to stay with an old lady?

The sheriff pulled into the drive of an old Victorian. The front door opened and a woman around seventy years of age stepped onto the front porch. A smile graced her face, her hands hidden in her apron.

"Inside, quick."

"Cowboys." Tracy froze, her gaze on the two men riding horses down the street.

"They'll patrol at regular intervals tonight." The sheriff grabbed a couple of bags, leaving the rest to Taya and led them quickly inside the house.

"June, meet Taya and Tracy. I'll send someone in the morning to pick them up."

"That's fine. We'll make cookies." She motioned down the hall. "You're welcome to the first room on the right. Bathroom is across the hall."

"Thank you. We really appreciate you letting us stay." Taya smiled.

"I love company. Even better with a spice of danger." She laughed and showed the sheriff out before turning back to Taya. "Y'all meet me in the kitchen when you're settled. You must be curious about the safe house."

Less than ten minutes later, Taya sat at a vintage

dinette set in the kitchen, a cup of coffee in front of her while June put Tracy to work baking oatmeal cookies. Things seemed so normal at the moment.

"You'll be staying in a house similar to this one, but also very different." June wagged her eyebrows. "The owner, Gemma O'Connor, formerly Ricca, bought the house when she ran away from her wedding. Being the daughter of a mob boss, and almost having married one, she built a safe room inside. You aren't the only ones who might have to use it." She held up the coffeepot.

"No, thanks. It's used regularly as a safe house?"

"First time that I know of. Last time someone had need of the place, Gemma rented it to them because her and her husband were traveling to Europe. I'm sure they'll take a vacation in order for you to stay there. Now that they're parents, they still want to help, but they won't put their family in danger."

"I understand that." She wished Tracy hadn't been put into danger. Taya had felt guilty enough when she'd been abducted while Taya was on a mission, but to find out that her partner, a man she trusted, was behind the abduction was almost too much to bear. There had to have been a clue she missed.

Rescuing Tracy and the other girls hadn't been the first such mission the group had been on. Had Mason been involved in those too? Had he simply gone along with the rescue to deflect suspicion off him? Men had died during those missions, both good and bad. How could she not have seen the type of man he was?

"Tell me about the cowboys." Tracy stirred the cookie mixture.

"Handsome, aren't they?" June dumped in some

chocolate chips. "The ranch they're from is fairly new. Usually, it's the motorcycle gang patrolling the streets when there's trouble, but they're away at some kind of rally. Sheriff Westbrook often asks for help from Langley PD, but the folks of Misty Hollow pitch in when needed. The two of you came to the right place."

"I thought so at first, but they still found us." Taya wrapped her hands around the coffee she had yet to take a sip of.

"Evil finds a way until good takes it out." June dropped spoonfuls of cookie dough onto a tray. "Bad people come to Misty Hollow, same as good. Happens more often than we'd like, to be honest." She waved the wooden spoon at Taya. "I can tell you this, though. We've yet to be beaten down or fail to send evil packing."

Taya was counting on it.

# Chapter Eighteen

A knock sounded on the door the next morning as Taya and Tracy enjoyed a breakfast of chocolate gravy and biscuits—something Tracy said she intended to eat every morning for the rest of her life.

"You go right ahead and get fat." Taya smiled and went to answer the door.

A police officer flashed his badge. "Langley PD. We're here to transfer you."

She glanced over at Tracy who shoved the last bite of biscuit into her mouth. "I'm ready." She jumped up and gave June a hug. "I promise to be back to visit when this is all over."

"I'll hold you to it." The woman returned the hug, then cupped her cheek. "We'll make a pie."

Tears shimmered in Tracy's eyes as she headed for the door and grabbed one of the bags sitting there. "I'm ready."

"It won't be long now." Taya tried to smile but failed.

"Right." Tracy shoved past her. "Let's get to our new prison."

"I've heard it's fancy." Taya grabbed the rest of the bags and followed the officer to the car waiting outside.

"The house is only a couple of blocks away," he said, opening the door for her. "You'll be there in no time."

"Thanks." She climbed into the backseat after Tracy and Betty.

A block away, a van blocked the road.

Taya dug her handgun from her backpack. "Whatever you do, don't leave my side."

The two officers exited the car, weapons drawn.

Shots rang out from the van, and they both fell.

Taya shoved her door open. "We've got to go. Now!" She yanked Tracy's arm. "Betty, run!" When the dog hesitated, she yelled again. "Tracy, they'll shoot her."

"Go, Betty." Her words broke on a sob. "Run!"

With a whine, the dog dashed behind the nearest house.

Taya grabbed Tracy's hand prepared to follow the dog.

Mason stepped from behind a massive magnolia tree. "Drop the gun and kick it over here, Taya, or I will shoot you. The girl is who I want. You're merely collateral damage."

"Hello, Mason." She dropped the gun and kicked it to him.

Sirens wailed in the distance. Good. Someone had heard the shots.

"We'd best be going, don't you think? Run to the van. Don't make me tell you twice."

Taya pushed Tracy ahead of her. "Do as he says."

A man opened the back doors before they got there, shoved them inside, and closed the door, thrusting them into darkness. A few seconds later, tires squealed away from the scene.

"I'm scared." Tracy sat as close to her as she could get without sitting on her lap.

"Me, too, but let's not lose our heads. See if you can find me a weapon. Anything hard or sharp." She felt around the carpeted floor. Nothing. The back of the van was empty.

"Where are they taking us?"

"Wherever they're hiding out, I suspect." She sat back against the wall and pulled Tracy close. "I won't let them take you away. I promise."

"You'll be outnumbered."

"I've been outnumbered before." Taya felt for her phone, relieved to find it still in her back pocket. She needed to find a place to hide it. Mason was sure to search her when they stopped. Further feeling around revealed nothing. Other than she and Tracy, the back of the van was empty.

"Ryan will never find us." Tracy's soft words fueled Taya's fear.

"Yes, he will. The sheriff put a tracker on my phone, remember? I'll drop it as soon as we're out of the van. It should take Mason's men a while before they find it." Hopefully, not before the sheriff discovered where they were taken.

It felt like maybe twenty minutes before the van stopped. Taya's heart leaped into her throat, Mason's words ringing through her head. If she was nothing more than collateral damage, why didn't he shoot her along with the two officers from Langley? He had to know she wouldn't go down easy.

The back doors opened. The morning sunlight

temporarily blinded her, and she stumbled as a man yanked her from the van. Pretending to need the van to stabilize herself, she slid the phone from her back pocket and dropped it, kicking it under the vehicle. Hopefully, it would be enough.

"Let's go." One man grabbed Taya, the other Tracy.

Mason strode ahead of them toward a large ranch-style farmhouse. "Put them in my office. Keep an eye on them. I'll be there in a minute. Take that van and grab the other girls. Stash them in the back room of the barn."

Taya's blood chilled. The man would drive over her phone, making it useless. She glanced back as he climbed into the driver's seat and pulled away. Taya could only imagine hearing the crunch of her phone on the gravel. There went her last hope of rescue. It was all on her now.

In an office of towering bookcases and polished cherrywood furniture, two burly men shoved them into armchairs and ordered them not to move. Their guards stood near the door. One grinned when Taya glanced his way.

She shuddered and turned back to Tracy. Her niece, skin pale, folded into herself, her face hidden by her hair. Soft whines came from her throat as she rocked back and forth.

Steel replaced the blood in Taya's veins. She would find a way to get them both out of here before Tracy suffered irreparable damage. Taya squared her shoulders and lifted her chin, then met the cold gaze of her guard with one of her own.

"The Boss is going to have fun with you," he

smirked out of the side of his mouth.

Taya kept her face impassive. She would not give him the satisfaction of showing fear.

The man's eyes widened. He frowned. "I'm not sure what he wants with a cold one like you, though."

"That is my concern." Mason stepped into the room. "Turn the chairs to face my desk, then you may wait outside. Close the door behind you." He sat.

Taya was lifted and turned as if she weighed nothing more than a small child. She switched her emotionless stare to the man she'd once called friend.

Mason grinned. "I bet you didn't think the man you looked for was me. Did you grieve when you thought I died? Ah. The flicker in your eyes tells me you did." He steepled his fingers. "I should win an award for my acting skills, don't you think? All those missions…I bet you're wondering why I turned. Simple answer, my dear Taya. Money. A crass reason, but true nevertheless." His brow furrowed. "So, it's the silent treatment. Shall I tell you what I plan to do with you and your pretty little niece?"

Taya swallowed against a throat as dry as the Sahara Desert and kept her gaze locked on a shadow on the wall caused by a tree branch outside. She didn't know how long she could keep her thoughts to herself, but she'd do so as long as possible.

"I guess you're wondering why you're here. Why I didn't kill you and take the girl." He shrugged. "I'm not exactly sure. Oh, your niece will fetch me a pretty penny, but you…well, you're just going to be trouble, aren't you? Unless—" His smile widened. "You think this through and see the benefits in joining me. We made a great team once; we could do so again."

Her gaze flicked to his. Join him? As in run a trafficking ring? Didn't he know her at all? If he had, he would know she would never do such a thing. She would die first.

"It might convince me to save your niece."

"Tracy." She forced her name through clenched lips. "Her name is Tracy."

"So, you haven't lost your ability to speak."

She hitched her chin again and looked slightly to her left.

"I must admit the top of a mountain is the last place I thought you'd flee." He got up and moved to the front of the desk where he perched a leg against it. "I thought you were more of a big-city gal." He leaned close, his breath on her face. "I found you, Taya. See, I know you better than you thought. I simply had to find your car. It didn't take too long after that. You hiked up the mountain, didn't you? Smart, but it didn't work. See?" He gripped her face in one hand and forced her to look at him. "You can't beat me."

She endured through the pain of having her cheeks smashed against her teeth. This was only the beginning.

~

"What do you mean you lost the signal?" Ryan whipped around from the window.

"I never had it. Just when I was zeroing in on it, it went out." Snowe glanced up from his laptop. "I don't know where they are."

"Let's be glad neither was shot along with the two Langley police officers." Sheriff Westbrook yanked open the front door.

Betty barged inside and made a beeline for Ryan. She barked and ran circles around him.

He knelt and wrapped his arms around her neck. "Do you think she can lead us to them?"

The sheriff shook his head. "Not if they were taken away in a vehicle, which I'm sure they were."

Ryan pushed to his feet. "I cannot believe they were taken one block from the safe house. How did Mason find them? Would June Mayfield have told anyone?"

"No way. That woman knows everything there is to know about everyone in this town, but she also knows how to keep a secret when she needs to. Otherwise, I wouldn't have put them with her." His face darkened.

"Sorry. I didn't mean to imply you don't know how to do your job." Ryan raked his fingers through his hair and plopped onto a chair. "They could be anywhere."

"Give me an hour," Snowe said. "I'll have a good idea. Within a mile at least."

"What if they don't have an hour?"

"Rogers won't move them right away. It'd be too risky. He's getting all his ducks in a row right now, so to speak." The sheriff sat across from him. "When we have a radius, we'll take the dog. She's a good bet at finding them."

Betty might be their only chance to find them. Ryan covered his face with his hands. They should've stayed with him on the mountaintop. Within twenty-four hours, Taya and Tracy were in the hands of a madman. One who didn't have any qualms about killing anyone who got between him and what he wanted.

Taya would definitely get between the man and

what he wanted. Ryan could only pray she'd hold back until he could save her. Then, he didn't care what she did to Mason Rogers.

The room fell silent except for the tapping of Snowe's fingers on the keyboard. No one had drifted through the woods or come close to the cabin since Taya had left. Ryan didn't think the sheriff had been seen taking the girls away, but who knew? Somehow, Rogers had discovered they were in town.

"Someone must have still been hiding in the woods." He pushed to his feet. "Mason left someone behind to watch the cabin. They saw Taya and Tracy leave." He snapped his fingers for his dogs to follow and headed for the back door. "They might still be there. Watching and relaying information back to Rogers. It's a long shot, but I'm going to check it out."

"Not alone." Sheriff Westbrook stood. "I doubt anyone is still out there, but it's best if I go with you. Agent Snowe, keep trying to locate our gals." He slapped his hat on his head.

Once they reached the tree line, Sheriff Westbrook put a finger to his lips as a signal for Ryan to be as quiet as possible. He nodded and whispered for the dogs to search. If someone was out there, Astro and Boris would find them. The dogs slinked into the brush, noses to the ground.

Even if his feeling was wrong about someone watching the cabin, activity was better than sitting around and doing nothing but worry about what was happening to Taya. They wouldn't harm Tracy. She was too valuable. But Taya—he shook his head.

A shout rang out ahead. Dogs growled.

Ryan and the sheriff sprinted toward the noise.

A man struggled out of his sleeping bag. On the ground next to him lay a high-tech listening device. Ryan was right.

This man had been listening to everything they said.

# Chapter Nineteen

**Mason released her** face and pulled a small black box from the top drawer of his desk before opening the door. "Put the girl with the others, then come back for the woman. She and I need to have a private conversation first."

Taya stared at the box in his hand, then at Tracy. "Do what they say, sweetie." Being compliant was her only chance.

"No. Taya!" Tracy showed the first signs of life since they arrived and stretched her arms for her aunt.

"Not to worry, I'll be fine. I'll find you in a bit."

"Touching." Mason grinned, then closed the door behind the man and Tracy. "You know we have ways of making people compliant." He leaned against his desk, ankles crossed, the box still in his hand. "Some ways more pleasant than others. Aren't you going to ask me why it matters whether you're compliant?"

"Okay, I'll bite. Why?" She again focused on a spot above his left shoulder, wishing more than anything she was in the landscape the portrait portrayed, sitting next to the creek with Ryan and Tracy. For now, she'd go there in her mind.

"I'm sure you remember our brief...relationship."

He tilted his head.

"There was no relationship."

"Well, I wanted there to be." He opened the box and pulled out a syringe. "Remember the man we needed to help us…to *want* to help us?"

She nodded. Her heart plummeted. Sweat broke out on her upper lip.

"A few doses of this, and he craved it. He'd do anything for it."

"What do you want, Mason?"

"You." He smiled and replaced the syringe. "I'll give you a few minutes to decide. Don't take too long. I'll be back in five."

The man was deranged. Taya could never condone what he was doing. She could never go along with trafficking young girls.

She eyed the black box. Would she really need what was in that syringe so desperately as to forget everything she fought for?

What if she said yes? Pretended? She stared at the carpet under her feet. Agreeing would give her an opportunity to save Tracy. That would be her condition even if she was lying. But, what about the others? She couldn't walk away and leave them; nor could she condone their being auctioned off like animals.

"Okay," she said, as the door opened behind her. "On one condition. Tracy is left alone."

"I'm afraid all agreements are off." A stony-faced Mason sat in his desk chair. He tossed what remained of her cell phone on the desk. "One of my men found this on the driveway. Of course, it's shattered. He took the sim card into the woods and disposed of it."

Her heart dropped.

"I'm wondering, though, whether the feds had time to track your location before we found the phone. It hadn't been long after your arrival."

"They'd be here by now if they'd tracked it."

He nodded. "I did consider that." He stared without speaking for several seconds before continuing. "It wounds be deeply that you'd forfeit what we could have for a few kids you don't even know."

"What you're doing is wrong."

"Is it? It's simply a form of slavery, Taya. Something that has been happening since the days of the pharaohs. Why should I not profit from it?" He tapped what was left of her phone. "No, I don't think anything short of violence will convince you to join me. Even that might not work."

She frowned. "Violence never solves anything."

"Spoken by one of the sharpest shooters the special ops group ever had." He laughed. "Your job was violence."

"For the greater good." She hadn't spared a second thought for taking down evil. Now, she sat across from a man every bit as bad as the ones she'd either killed or handed over to law enforcement. "Violence or drugs won't work on me. I'm trained against it, Mason."

"But, it'll be fun to try." He grinned. "Something for me to look back on when I need a boost." He yelled for someone named Bill to enter. "Take her to the barn. You know what to do. Come get me when it's done. In the meantime, the others will prepare to move. Again." He shot her a harsh look as Bill yanked her to her feet.

"I love the barn." Bill's grip on her arm tightened.

"Good for you. Glad I can accommodate."

"I'll enjoy knocking that smart mouth around."

"Ah. So, you're his muscle." Dear God, the man was a mountain. All Taya needed to do was stay alive until help arrived, which might be harder than she thought.

They passed several outbuildings. Which one held Tracy and the girls? Maybe they were in the house. She stifled a sigh and glanced toward the road. Where was her help?

Once in the barn, Bill gave her a shove that almost brought her to her knees. She managed to stay on her feet and turned. "Will you undo my hands so I have a fighting chance, or are you afraid I might beat you?"

He laughed. "A tiny thing like you? Sure. I'll release you. It'll be more fun than beating up someone who can't defend themselves, and The Boss didn't say I had to keep you tied up."

The instant her hands were free, she jumped back. Every instinct told her to run. Her brain told her she'd never make it before he caught her. Fighting her way free was her only chance and a poor one at that. She'd need every bit of training she possessed.

Taya didn't see his fist coming. A sharp right hook knocked her back two steps. A well-aimed kick sent her to her knees. With a primal yell, she charged, wrapping her arms around his waist.

He picked her up and tossed her like a sack of grain.

She hit the wall with a heavy thud. The breath escaped her in a rush.

"This is fun." He aimed another punch.

She ducked, whirling as his fist connected with the wall.

He cursed and spun to face her. "You might be

fast, little girl, but I'm stronger."

Staying out of his reach was her only chance. As she danced on the balls of her feet, she glanced around for a weapon. A shovel sat propped in a corner. A sledgehammer hung from a hook. A pitchfork stuck out of a bale of hay. Plenty of weapons and all too far for her to reach. Still, she had to try.

She dove for the closest. The pitchfork.

"Nice try." Bill tackled her to the ground.

Her head hit the hard-packed dirt floor. She wrapped her legs around him and squeezed.

Grunting, he rolled and threw a punch, catching her in the side of her head.

Stars swam in front of her eyes. Another punch and she tasted blood.

She scrambled back, her breath coming in gasps. She spit, then smiled and wiggled her fingers for him to come. When he stepped close, she threw a roundhouse kick to his head.

He staggered back. "Good one." With a roar, he charged, again lifting her off her feet and slamming her into the next bale of hay. She slid to the floor like a rag doll.

"What's the purpose of this?" She managed to say past her split lip. "Why not kill me?"

He jerked his head to a corner. "The Boss enjoys watching. Say cheese, you're being filmed."

Taya glared at the camera high in the corner and vowed she wouldn't fight anymore. She wouldn't give him the satisfaction of seeing her knocked around, fighting vainly for her life until this brute finished her off. She closed her eyes and waited for the next punch.

~

"Got it!" Snowe jumped to his feet. "The last ding on the phone came from these woods." He tapped the screen. "No buildings, but it's a start. If we send a chopper into the air, we're bound to find them. This man has too many men to hide effectively from anyone searching from the air."

"I'm going with you." Ryan tucked his handgun into the waistband of his jeans. Although he'd never shot anyone before, he figured he could if he had Mason in his sights. "What if we spot them?"

"We find a place to land out of sight, then storm the place. Backup will be waiting." Agent Larson opened the front door. "The dogs have to stay behind."

"Sorry, guys. A helicopter is no place for dogs." Ryan patted both their heads, praying he'd see his furry friends again. *Hold on, Taya. We're coming.*

Sheriff Westbrook clapped Ryan on the shoulder. "You sure you're up to this? Things could get ugly."

"I can do this for Taya and Tracy." He squared his shoulders.

"This isn't a scene in a book, Ryan."

"I'm aware of that. You can't keep me from going."

"Sure, I can." The sheriff met his gaze for a moment, then shrugged. "I'd do the same thing under the circumstances. You follow my orders, got it?"

Ryan nodded as relief flooded through him. "Absolutely."

"Right." He turned and followed the agents.

An hour later, far too long in Ryan's opinion, they were finally in the air. So much could've happened in the time since Taya and Tracy were taken. His mind spun with scenarios, and none of them were good. This was not a good time to be a suspense writer.

The pilot took them directly to the last spot the phone dinged then flew in increasing circles with each pass. The fifth pass took them over a large farm buzzing with men and several vehicles.

"We found them." Agent Larson waved his hand. "Fly to a safe place to land. We don't want them fleeing before we can get to them. Contact our backup and tell them where to meet us."

Ryan wiped sweaty palms on his jeans. This was it. Please, God, let them reach the farm in time to save Taya and Tracy.

The pilot landed in a field approximately two miles from the farm. "We hoof it from here," Snowe said. "Make it quick. Rogers and his men have been warned. They won't have missed the chopper."

This all took too long. Too long to locate the phone. Too long to get in the air. Too long to hike to the farm. Despair welled in Ryan. He felt completely inadequate for the task ahead of him and could only pray the sheriff and the agents would be enough.

They trekked single file through the thick brush, following the railroad tracks for ease of movement. No one spoke. Tension rolled off them like waves of humidity shimmering in the air.

Sheriff Westbrook tossed Ryan a bottle of water.

He guzzled half of it before stuffing it in the pack he'd been given when they'd exited the helicopter. A pack full of guns and ammo. A pack ready for a war he was ill-equipped for. What he could do was be there for Taya once she was rescued. He forced himself to remain positive that she and Tracy were still alive.

Larson held up a hand for them to halt.

Sounds of movement came from the other side of a stand of trees. It seemed as if the ring of traffickers was packing up to leave. Maybe the agents had caught them before they could prepare to stand and fight.

"Target spotted." Snowe stepped back from his viewing place. "Rogers has headed for the barn. There's a back door. We'll go in that way once the coast is clear."

Ryan closed his eyes and prayed.

# Chapter Twenty

The opening of the barn door brought Taya back to consciousness. At the sound of Mason's voice, she rolled behind the hay bale. Every movement made her breath hitch, and she fought to control her breathing so the two men wouldn't hear her.

"Is she dead?" Mason asked.

"She ain't moved in a while."

Mason exhaled heavily. "Pity. You can go now. We'll be leaving as soon as possible."

"What about her?"

"Leave her."

Taya's heart thudded. At least she was alive enough to feel each sharp stab of pain.

Soft footsteps came her way as the barn door opened again. Inch by inch, Taya pushed to a sitting position.

"So, you aren't dead." Mason grinned down at her. "You are the strongest woman I've ever met."

She spit, blood dotting his boots. "Thanks for the compliment."

He hunkered down next to her. "You don't look good, Taya."

"Thanks again."

"What should I do with you now?"

"I'm at your mercy." She took a quick glance at the pitchfork sticking up from the bale.

"I could leave you here to suffer through your injuries. Eventually you'd succumb to them." He brushed a strand of damp hair out of her eyes. "But you'd live the last few hours of your life knowing Tracy was out of your reach forever."

Her stomach rolled. She turned her head and wretched.

Pushing to his feet, Mason shook his head. "A real pity."

When he turned, she lunged to the other side of the hay bale, drawing on every last bit of strength she could muster and gripped the pitchfork. "Hey, Mason."

He whirled, pulling a gun from his waistband.

She thrust her weapon forward, ramming the sharp points into his gut. "You'll spend what little time you have left knowing you've failed." She shoved it deeper.

He fell, taking the pitchfork with him and dropping his weapon. Obscenities spewed from his mouth as he tried to pull the fork free. "This time I'll make sure you die by my hand."

"Good luck with that." Taya stumbled for the door, grabbing Mason's dropped Glock on her way. She peered out the double doors. No one paid any attention to the barn. She stepped out. When no cry of alarm came, she ran for the nearest building, a metal shed that looked as if it was used to hold heavy machinery.

The massive front doors refused to budge. Taya skirted around the corner, one hand clutching the gun, the other arm held tight to her ribcage. Every breath ripped through her, a shudder letting her know something inside was broken. No time for healing now. She'd check out her injuries once Tracy was safe.

A side door slid open with the shriek of metal on metal. Taya glanced back to see whether she had attracted any attention. When no one dashed her way, she slipped inside, sliding the door closed behind her.

Darkness greeted her. Where was a flashlight when a girl needed one?

Her shin banged something hard. She hissed against the pain and kept moving toward a small light from under a door on the opposite side of the building.

Taya pressed her ear to the panel. "Tracy?" She knocked three times.

"We're here, Taya. We're here."

Tears stung as she fought to open the locked door. "Hold on. I need to find a way to break in. How many of you are in there?"

"Six counting me."

Taya shoved the Glock into her waistband and stretched her arm in front of her, sweeping the air for anything that would help her open that door. She felt the wall on each side of the door. Her fingers brushed a ring of keys dangling from a hook.

Bingo. Thank you, Lord.

The side door screeched. She ducked, holding her breath, pulling the weapon.

"You can't take the girls yet, Bill."

"Why not?"

"The Boss hasn't given the order."

"He said we're fixin' to clear out. We can't do that without the girls."

"Dude, I'd ask him first. You know how he gets."

Bill cursed. "Fine." The door slid closed, casting

her once more into darkness.

She didn't have much time. There was no help coming. This was all on her.

The fifth key she tried unlocked the door. She yanked it open. "Tracy?"

Something hit her in the back of the head, driving her to her knees. The keys fell from her hand. The gun skittered across the floor. A pretty red-haired girl promptly sat on it.

Taya glanced back to see Bill's grinning face.

"Imagine seeing you again. I hope The Boss gives me another go at taking you down." He snatched up the keys and slammed the door.

Tracy launched herself at Taya, dropping to her knees beside her. "You're hurt."

"A little bit." Taya scooted against the wall to catch her breath. "I'll be fine. Nothing a little rest can't fix."

"Is Ryan coming?"

"Sure, he is." She really hoped so and prayed he was bringing the cavalry. "May I have the gun, please?"

The girl slid it to her. "How are you going to get us out of here since you're locked up too?"

"With this." She laid the gun in her lap and rested her head on the wall behind her. "Everyone okay?"

"Yes." Tracy sat beside her and rested her head on Taya's shoulder. "I knew you'd come. I knew they couldn't kill you."

They almost had. Still might, but she'd fight to her last breath to keep these girls from being sold and used. She just had to hold on until help came.

"You don't look so good," Tracy said.

"That's the second time I've been told that today."

Her eyes drifted closed.

"Don't go to sleep." Tracy shook her.

"That hurts."

"Sorry, but we need you."

"I'm not going anywhere." She opened her eyes and cupped her niece's face. "I need to rest for what's coming. While I do, is there anything in this room you girls can use to defend yourselves?"

"Susy is wearing combat boots. Allison is wearing heels, but that's it."

"Then use those. They're better than nothing."

The girls grouped together, removing the heavier shoes, and formed a line in front of Taya.

"Don't block my aim of the door."

They shifted to give her room to fire at anyone who showed their face.

~

Ryan followed the others from the trees to the back of the barn. They slipped inside one by one.

"Got one down." Snowe stood over a man with a pitchfork in his stomach. "It's Mason Rogers."

The man groaned. "Help me."

"Where's Taya Trapp?" The sheriff glared down at him. "Where are the girls?"

"No idea where Taya is. She tried to kill me and ran. The girls are in the equipment building. Call an ambulance."

"Sure thing, buddy. Once the girls are free and your men rounded up." Sheriff Westbrook nodded at the others. "Don't go out there, guns blazing. Our backup is coming from the other direction. We'll herd these men to the center of the front yard. Don't shoot unless you have to. Boyne, you and Larson, find those girls."

Good. That would be a lot better than the shootout he figured the others couldn't avoid. He spared Rogers a glance. "Want me to call an ambulance?"

"Yes. Just in case someone else is injured." The sheriff peered out the wide double doors.

Ryan placed the call to 911, verified the address, told them he couldn't stay on the line, and then hung up as Larson darted out the way they'd come. Ryan rushed out after him.

Gunshots rang out from the front of the barn. So much for a peaceful roundup.

Larson pointed to a large metal building.

Ryan nodded, his heart in his throat. *Taya, where are you?*

A man came around the corner and aimed at his forehead.

Larson fired and dropped him where he stood. "I'll keep watch. Open that door."

Ryan pulled the side door open, wincing at the shrill shriek, then ducked inside. Larson backed in and unclicked a flashlight from his belt.

"Doesn't look like anything's in here but tractors." Ryan followed the light's beam.

"Over there. A door." Larson shot another man who tried barging into the building.

Larson rushed to the other side of the building and turned the knob. Locked. "I need the light."

Larson tossed the flashlight to him. To Ryan's surprise, he caught it as it spun end over end in his direction. He shined the stream of light on the walls, locating a key ring on a hook. *Come on. Work.* It took him three tries before he found the right key. He yanked the door open.

A line of girls holding shoes above their heads screamed and rushed him. A bullet whizzed past his head as he stumbled back.

"Wait. I'm one of the good guys." He held up his hands.

"Ryan?" Tracy dropped the book she held and jumped, wrapping arms and legs around him, driving him backward into a tractor.

"Hmmph." He set her on her feet. "Where's Taya?"

"Inside. She's hurt pretty bad."

His heart dropped to his feet as he pushed past the line of girls.

There wasn't a place on Taya's face that wasn't covered in either bruises or blood. He dropped to his knees. "Oh, baby." He took the gun from her hand and gathered her into his arms. "Let's get you out of here." Placing one arm behind her and another under her knees, he lifted her into his arms, kissing her temple. "An ambulance is coming."

"Mason is in the barn."

"I saw him. Is he the one who did this?"

"No. He ordered one of his men to do it." She nestled her head into the crook of his shoulder. "That one." She pointed to one of the men lying outside the building.

"Then, I'm glad Larson shot him."

"Man, she doesn't look good." Larson frowned. "Ambulance just arrived. Have them take her before Rogers."

"He isn't dead?" She lifted her head.

"No, ma'am. You the one who used the

pitchfork?" Larson's mouth twitched.

"Guilty." She tried to smile, then groaned. "I wanted him to suffer."

"I'm sure you're getting your wish."

Ryan carried her past a stretcher that held Mason, minus the pitchfork. "Want to say anything to him before he's wheeled away? It's probably your last chance."

"Yes, but I want to be standing when I do."

He slowly placed her on her feet and stood close enough to catch her if she started to fall.

"You failed, Mason." She lifted her chin. "If you survive your wounds, you'll spend the rest of your life behind bars. Do you know what they do to child molesters in prison? Of course, you do. You once fought for the good side. I'd wish you luck, but you deserve everything you get."

"Come on, sweetheart." Ryan put an arm around her waist. "Let's get you checked out." He glanced into the pale face of evil, then turned away. The man didn't warrant his attention. Once outside, he reluctantly handed Taya over to the paramedics, then glanced around for the girls. They huddled near the front porch. Catching sight of Tracy sitting on the top step, tears streaming down her face, he headed her way.

"Is she going to die?" She swiped her arm across her eyes.

"I don't think so, but she'll need us to take care of her for a while."

"I'll do anything. She's saved me twice, Ryan." She raised red eyes to his. "I can never repay her for that."

"Oh, sweetie." He sat next to her and took her

hands in his. "She won't expect you to. Taya saved you because she loves you. She saved these other girls because she fights on the side of justice. Your aunt is a pretty special woman."

Tracy gave him a shaky smile. "You going to make your fake marriage official?"

He chuckled. "If she'll have me. So, what was up with the shoes?"

"They're the only weapons we had. Taya told us to fight with all we had." She leaned against him. "I want to be like her when I grow up."

"You're already more like her than you know."

# Epilogue

**Three days later**, Taya limped up the steps to Ryan's cabin, his arm around her waist supporting her. Bruises, contusions, a concussion, and two broken ribs had kept her in a hospital bed for three days too long. All she wanted was to be home. Home being this cabin on top of Misty Mountain.

Ryan helped her to the sofa. "Can I bring you anything?"

"I can make sandwiches." Tracy rushed to the kitchen.

"No, I'm fine, really." She held out a hand to him. "Sit with me."

"Nothing I'd rather do." He sat and gently pulled her to his side. "Your face is a nice array of chartreuse and eggplant."

"You do know how to flatter a girl." She smiled and nestled into him. "I feel better now that I'm home."

The crunch of gravel outside alerted him to company. "My guess is that's Sheriff Westbrook coming to tell us what happened that day." Ryan only knew what he'd seen for himself. A gunfight and a rescue.

Since Ryan had left the door open to allow the late

spring breeze to blow through, the sheriff knocked and entered, removing his hat. He smiled in Taya's direction. "Nice to see you back."

"It's great to be back." She scooted to sit upright. "News?"

He nodded, his smile fading. "Mason Rogers succumbed to his injuries last night. The men we managed to round up that were still breathing have been taken to await trial."

"The girls?"

"All safely home with their families." His serious gaze locked with hers. "You are a remarkable woman, Taya Trapp. If you ever want to work in law enforcement, please consider my department. We'd be lucky to have you."

"Thank you, but I think I'll continue saving the innocent."

"Then you let me know if you ever need my help." He replaced his hat. "I do hope you'll stick around. All three of you." With a nod, he left the way he'd come.

"I'd like that." She glanced up at Ryan. "To stick around."

"You would?" He ran his thumb gently over her bruised jaw. "Because I'd like nothing better than for you and Tracy to stay here with me permanently. I made an offer on this cabin, and the owner accepted. Will you marry me for real this time?"

"Yes." She offered a crooked smile and a wince. "As soon as these bruises fade, and I can take a deep breath without gasping. I want to marry you right outside, standing in the yard at sunset, the dogs around us, Tracy at my side."

"Sounds perfect." He lowered his head and gently

caressed her split lips. "Waiting until you're healed sounds good since I plan on kissing you hard and long."

"Oh, really?" Her eyes blurred with tears.

"Absolutely. And I want your gasping to be something other than pain."

"Hush. Tracy will hear you." She laughed, resting her forehead on his chest.

"Please. I know what married people do. Don't forget what you saved me from." Tracy set a plate with three peanut butter and jelly sandwiches on the table. "We need to go shopping."

*We*. That simple two-letter word had never held more meaning than in that moment. "Yes, we do. You and I need some nice dresses." She leaned back against Ryan, not wanting to be anywhere else but right there.

The End

Dear Reader,

I hope you've enjoyed the Misty Hollow series. While *Mountain Refuge* might be the last of these, another series set in Misty Hollow is coming. The Cowboys of Misty Hollow, a new series of romantic suspense featuring some of the same characters you've come to know and love.

I hope you'll grab *Cowboy Peril,* book one when it's available. Maybe you'll fall in love at first sight with the brave cowboys just as young Tracy did.

If you enjoyed *Mountain Refuge*, please go to Amazon and leave a review. Reviews are very important to an author and help other readers find the very books you enjoyed.

God Bless,

Cynthia

www.cynthiahickey.com

Cynthia Hickey is a multi-published and best-selling author of cozy mysteries and romantic suspense. She has taught writing at many conferences and small writing retreats. She and her husband run the publishing press, Winged Publications. They live in Arizona and Arkansas, becoming snowbirds with three dogs. They have ten grandchildren who keep them busy and tell everyone they know that "Nana is a writer."

Connect with me on FaceBook
Twitter
Sign up for my newsletter and receive a free short story
www.cynthiahickey.com

Follow me on Amazon
And Bookbub
Shop my bookstore on shopify. For better prices and autographed books.

Enjoy other books by Cynthia Hickey

**Misty Hollow**
Secrets of Misty Hollow
Deceptive Peace
Calm Surface
Lightning Never Strikes Twice

Lethal Inheritance
Bitter Isolation
Say I Don't
Christmas Stalker
Bridge to Safety


Stay in Misty Hollow for a while. Get the entire series here!

**The Seven Deadly Sins series**
Deadly Pride
Deadly Covet
Deadly Lust
Deadly Glutton
Deadly Envy
Deadly Sloth
Deadly Anger


**The Tail Waggin' Mysteries**
Cat-Eyed Witness
The Dog Who Found a Body
Troublesome Twosome
Four-Legged Suspect
Unwanted Christmas Guest
Wedding Day Cat Burglar


**Brothers Steele**
Sharp as Steele
Carved in Steele
Forged in Steele
Brothers Steele (All three in one)


**The Brothers of Copper Pass**

Wyatt's Warrant
Dirk's Defense
Stetson's Secret
Houston's Hope
Dallas's Dare
Seth's Sacrifice
Malcolm's Misunderstanding
The Brothers of Copper Pass Boxed Set

**Time Travel**
The Portal

**Tiny House Mysteries**
No Small Caper
Caper Goes Missing
Caper Finds a Clue
Caper's Dark Adventure
A Strange Game for Caper
Caper Steals Christmas
Caper Finds a Treasure
Tiny House Mysteries boxed set

**Wife for Hire – Private Investigators**
Saving Sarah
Lesson for Lacey
Mission for Meghan
Long Way for Lainie
Aimed at Amy
Wife for Hire (all five in one)

**A Hollywood Murder**

Killer Pose, book 1
Killer Snapshot, book 2
Shoot to Kill, book 3
Kodak Kill Shot, book 4
To Snap a Killer
Hollywood Murder Mysteries

**Shady Acres Mysteries**
Beware the Orchids, book 1
Path to Nowhere
Poison Foliage
Poinsettia Madness
Deadly Greenhouse Gases
Vine Entrapment
Shady Acres Boxed Set

**CLEAN BUT GRITTY Romantic Suspense**

**Highland Springs**

Murder Live
Say Bye to Mommy
To Breathe Again
Highland Springs Murders (all 3 in one)

**Colors of Evil Series**

Shades of Crimson
Coral Shadows

**The Pretty Must Die Series**

CYNTHIA HICKEY

Ripped in Red, book 1
Pierced in Pink, book 2
Wounded in White, book 3
Worthy, The Complete Story

**Lisa Paxton Mystery Series**

Eenie Meenie Miny Mo
Jack Be Nimble
Hickory Dickory Dock
Boxed Set

Hearts of Courage
A Heart of Valor
The Game
Suspicious Minds
After the Storm
Local Betrayal
Hearts of Courage Boxed Set

Overcoming Evil series
Mistaken Assassin
Captured Innocence
Mountain of Fear
Exposure at Sea
A Secret to Die for
Collision Course
Romantic Suspense of 5 books in 1

**INSPIRATIONAL**

**Nosy Neighbor Series**
Anything For A Mystery, Book 1
A Killer Plot, Book 2
Skin Care Can Be Murder, Book 3
Death By Baking, Book 4
Jogging Is Bad For Your Health, Book 5
Poison Bubbles, Book 6
A Good Party Can Kill You, Book 7
Nosy Neighbor collection

Christmas with Stormi Nelson

**The Summer Meadows Series**
Fudge-Laced Felonies, Book 1
Candy-Coated Secrets, Book 2
Chocolate-Covered Crime, Book 3
Maui Macadamia Madness, Book 4
All four novels in one collection

**The River Valley Mystery Series**
Deadly Neighbors, Book 1
Advance Notice, Book 2
The Librarian's Last Chapter, Book 3
All three novels in one collection